KEEPING THE HUMAN'S HEART

TROLLKIN LOVERS BOOK FIVE

LYONNE RILEY

Introduction

Esme will not be used again, certainly not as fodder in war. When she makes a mad dash from the field of battle, she becomes a deserter, with nowhere to go except deeper into trollkin territory.

Drazak the orc and Han'zir the troll have lived a quiet, peaceful life together on their farm—until they find a human woman sleeping in their barn. When Esme convinces them to let her stay in exchange for work, Han'zir is excited about their new "pet" human. But Drazak is inexplicably drawn to her, and fears what his hunger could mean for them when Han'zir has already refused his bonding pledge once before.

It's not long before Esme begins to feel at home in this idyllic place. But she'll soon find she can't escape the war forever.

Content Warnings

May contain spoilers!

- Graphic depictions of sex: M/M, M/F, and M/M/F
- Anal play and anal sex

- Double penetration, spit-roasting, and double missionary
- Breeding
- War and wartime themes
- Hunger and starvation
- Violence and death
- Mild gore
- Death of multiple animals (off-page)
- Hunting of animals for survival
- Mercy killing of an animal
- Emotional and physical abuse (in the past)
- Physical assault
- Arson
- Pregnancy
- Birth
- Lactation play

CHAPTER 1

ESME

"L ine up!" calls out the major. He paces in front of us, hands behind his back. We've only been in training for a week. Soon we'll be sent to the front lines as bait, meant to draw the trollkin out of their well-defended town so the archers and catapults behind us can destroy them. That's the only purpose we serve.

"Keep your heads high!" he roars. "For the King!"

"For the King!" we echo back, because not saying it means a stick to the knees.

I peek at the men and women standing to either side of me, dressed in the thickest clothes they could find. We weren't given armor, and the only weapon I have is the small axe I brought with me from the master's house. Before all of this I was a maid, a cook, a nanny. I watched over his children and chopped the wood and made the meals. Now the major is asking me to charge into battle and kill any trollkin I encounter in cold blood.

Little do they know that I'm a coward.

"Why are they even bothering to train us?" asks a redheaded woman around the fire that night. She has pale, freckled skin, but it's hard to tell which dots are freckles and which are mud. Everything is muddy with the constant rain. "We're just going to die anyway. That's all we're good for."

I wrap my arms around myself and shiver. The moment we're sent into battle, we're corpses on legs.

"Maybe we'll take out a trollkin or two before we go," says a taller man, a handsome one who seems to be her friend.

Her green eyes are sharp. "Just because you *can* kill, doesn't mean you should."

He snorts. "You're the one with a weakness for them, not me."

The woman growls at him in warning, and I wonder what he meant.

After the others go to bed, it's just me and her staring into the flames, wondering what will happen in the battle tomorrow.

"I'm Telise, by the way," the redhead says, holding out a hand. When we shake, though, my fingers are trembling. She gives me a look of pity. "You're not a fighter, are you?"

I shake my head. "I'm a maid."

She sighs. "Don't listen to Deleran. It's not about killing—it's about surviving. Do whatever you have to do in order to live." Her gaze slides off into the trees, like she's thinking about something far away. "The trollkin don't want to be here, either."

I tilt my head. "They want our land. They attacked us because they love war."

"Did they? Or are we the ones attacking them tomorrow?" Telise leans back, tilting her head up toward the night sky. "See, little maid, it's just a matter of perspective. They're not what you think they are."

My brow furrows. "What do you mean? They're monsters."

But she just shakes her head like I'm a child with much to learn about the world. "Not at all. I'd say they're a lot like us, and we have more in common than we realize."

Something sad lies behind the words, as if there's a whole layer I'm missing. But she doesn't seem inclined to speak further, so I tell her goodnight and stumble back to my bedroll, knowing I won't be able to sleep.

The next day, the major herds us into formation, and in the shuffle I lose track of Telise. Damn. She'd seen a few different battles and lived through them, so I thought staying close to her might mean surviving this.

Once again, I'm on my own.

When we step out of the trees, the high, wooden walls of the trollkin town loom above us. We're supposed to invade this place? I can't see how we could possibly hope to take it.

The moment we appear, arrows rain down on us—some of them even on fire. All around me, the screaming begins, and my fellow soldiers are already falling.

I have to get out of here. That's the only thing I know for certain.

The big front gates of the city open, and the huge, green and blue bodies of trollkin stream out. They're much stronger than we are, with cruel tusks curving out of their mouths and bright red and yellow eyes. All it takes is a cursory glance to see that unlike us, they're actually outfitted for war, dressed in helmets and metal chainmail.

Pain rips through my arm. An arrow is lodged in my bicep, and my own scream joins the cacophony. But I don't let myself fall. I can't, or I'm dead the moment those trollkin are on top of us.

Tears stream down my face as I pull the arrow out of my flesh. My blood pumping hot and fast, I turn and bolt. Not back towards the trees, because one of the officers lined up behind us would easily clock me for desertion, and execute me on the spot. Instead, I run to one side, past the other conscripted all charging into battle. How do they have that kind of courage? I can't fathom it. This agony in my arm is enough for me, thank you very much.

Dodging other humans, I race along the wall of the town, close enough that the arrows aren't falling on top of me. At least I've always been quick on my feet, ready to run at a moment's notice if the master got that look in his eye that said he needed to vent his anger. I know how to make an escape and stay gone as long as I need to.

Someone shouts at me to stop, but I ignore them just as I ignore the screams and bleeding bodies. If I can keep moving, maybe I'll avoid an arrow or gunshot and make it out of this alive. I have to keep going.

Finally, I reach the edge of the town, where the human forces are spread thinner. A big woman sits on a horse, and she's certainly higher up on the food chain than I am. She's the one who notices me making a break for it, and she doesn't think twice before she pulls out her gun and aims it at me.

I drop and roll as the shot echoes in the air. It's idiotic to be wasting shots on me when she could be shooting at the wave of trollkin headed straight for us, but the King's army has no pity for deserters. I tumble and leap back into a run, and while she's busy packing another bullet, I set foot over the tree line. It'll be much harder for her or anyone else to take aim at me in here.

My lungs burn, and hot blood streams down my arm, but I can't think about that right now. I keep my eyes on the forest ahead of me, trying not to barrel into a shrub or a tree trunk. My legs are wearing out, and soon my body is slowing and my chest is heaving.

No. I have to keep going. If I can get out of this place, if I can leave the scent of burning flesh behind, I'll be safe. The noise of swords and gunshots fades behind me, and yet I continue running, gritting my teeth and pressing my hand down over my wound to staunch the flow of blood.

What am I going to do about this once I do get out of here? The only place I could find medical supplies is the human military camp, but if I show my face there, they'll know I deserted and I won't live to see another day anyway. Or, perhaps worse, I'll simply end up on the front lines again.

Better to take the risk and hope it heals on its own.

Not that I have any idea where I'll go now. I'm deep in the woods, making sure to leave a wide berth between my path and the camp. Once I'm certain the woman on the horse won't follow me, I slow down to a ragged walk.

Clenching my jaw through the pain in my arm, I trudge on as the sun gets lower in the sky. When it's finally too dark for me to see any longer, I lie down on the bare forest floor and try to sleep, but the pain keeps me awake. The night is cold and I hug myself tight, trying to warm up. For hours I lay there, sobbing and then running out of tears again, until the sun comes back up. If I slept, I don't remember it.

Then I'm plodding on again. Walking and walking through endless woods, occasionally crossing a river or passing through a meadow. What could I possibly find out here? I don't even know where I am. This could be trollkin territory, where I could encounter their soldiers at any time. Or is it human territory now? I don't know anymore.

We're just pawns moving on a board between the King and the Grand Chieftain, back and forth, spilling more blood.

Useless cow, my master's voice echoes in my head. Once again I'm an object to be tossed around, to be used and abused as higher powers see fit.

It's afternoon when the trees abruptly give way. I'm up on a hill, a sharp slope leading down into a valley. A big river runs through the middle, probably big enough that I wouldn't be able to cross without getting swept away. The grasses are a summer yellow, but beyond that is green.

A farm. Row after row of bright green vegetables and stalks of corn. *Food.*

I didn't realize just how hungry I was until I gaze upon this bounty, but now it's like a vast hole has appeared in me that desires nothing more than to be filled. My panic and adrenaline have given way to this one need, and I rush down the slope.

The farm is a lot farther away than it looked, so I don't reach the edge of the field until it's almost sunset and the sky is stippled purple and orange. I honestly can't say if it's a human farm or a trollkin one. I have no clue where I am or how far I've gone since the battle began.

I follow the edge of the field, keeping just inside the tall vegetable stalks so no one can spot me from a distance. I search for something ripe to eat, but there's only raw wheat here. Damn. I press on until a building appears.

It's crafted with wood and thatch, but in such an odd shape that it must be trollkin-made. Great. I'm right in the middle of enemy territory, like I'd feared. If I'm discovered, I might face a death even worse than desertion. And yet I need somewhere to sleep that isn't the forest floor if I'm to keep going. I don't know where I'm headed, but anywhere beyond that battlefield is better.

Approaching the building quietly, I keep to the shadows as the sunlight fades. The barn is attached to a big pen, and axes designed specifically for butchering hang from the walls. I shudder.

Inside the barn it's empty and dark. The chickens squawk as I investigate, but there doesn't seem to be anyone around.

Good. I need a real place to rest, somewhere I can get just one night's sleep. There are a few apples tucked in a basket, likely intended for horses, and I grab as many as I can carry. I squeeze past the chickens and find a ladder leading upward to a second floor filled with hay.

Perfect.

I build a little nest out of the hay, then dive into the first apple. Oh, it's bliss. Juice slips down my chin, but I don't care. After devouring one, I eat another, then another. When I'm full, I lie back in the hay, relishing how even as the straw bites into my back, at least it's not the forest floor.

I'll take it, even with the fiery ache in my arm.

That night, I don't even dream.

Drazak

That damn troll.

The chickens squawked like hell last night, but he refused to go look. "If it's a coyote or a wolf," Han'zir said, "it's already done the deed."

"We need to get a dog," I'd snapped. Something to bark and scare off those mangy pests. We've only got a handful of cows and an even smaller handful of chickens, but without them, we've got no breakfast, and I can't function without a big breakfast. Eggs, ham from that pig farmer down the way, and sometimes a piece of bread if I've had the sense to make any. Han'zir doesn't bake, or really cook at all. He's pretty useless, I'd say, but he's good at pulling weeds, and the crops are only flourishing because of his green thumb. He knows when they need water, when they should be trimmed back, when the last freeze is coming so we can get ready to plant. He has a kind of knowing about things like that, and I've learned not to doubt his instincts.

"You know I hate dogs," Han'zir complains, slathering his bread with butter before downing it.

"You're lucky you have a nice ass," I tell him, slapping it as I get up out of my chair. He yelps, then gives me a wicked smile that pulls one of his tusks up on the side of his mouth. My troll likes it when I talk just a little foul, but I have too many things to do this morning to bend him over the table and shove my cock into him.

Or be the one bent over the table. That might be even better today, but perhaps later.

I shake my head as I head out the back door. I have to check the irrigation, then collect the chicken eggs. It's almost time to pull up potatoes and probably even the carrots. We want to plant a new batch before we switch over to turnips and parsnips this winter to restore some nutrients to the soil.

By the time I get to the barn, the sun is getting high in the sky, and I have to block it out with one arm. Today's going to be a hot one, which should be good for the peppers. The spicier ones have sold well lately, so we doubled our crop this year. Never thought I'd be making my profit bringing seasoning to the masses.

I check the first nest, and find no eggs inside. That's odd. The chickens are all alive and accounted for, so I guess there wasn't a latenight visitor. The next nest is empty, too.

Maybe a weasel? All the nests have been cleared out, which irritates me. I'm not going to have eggs for breakfast tomorrow at this rate.

That's when I spot a white eggshell. Someone or something has eaten my precious breakfast and left behind the evidence.

I search the rest of the barn, but find nothing else of note. I wonder what came through last night that took all the eggs but didn't disturb the chickens. It all strikes me as very odd.

We really should get a dog, whether Han'zir likes it or not. I'd never admit it to him, but I'd welcome the companionship as I do my chores every day. It would love us unconditionally, and bring vibrance to a life that can sometimes feel stale.

After I finish milking the cows, I find my troll checking on the vegetables and pulling out all the choice-looking greens. He must be planning a trip into town.

"All the eggs are gone," I tell him, and he jumps.

"I told you not to walk up on me like that," he says, setting aside his project. "They're just... gone?"

As if in acknowledgment of this crime, my stomach grumbles. "Yep. Left nothing but an eggshell."

He rubs his chin thoughtfully. "Haven't seen that one before."

Neither have I. And the mystery remains unsolved.

That night I cook up something good, using one of the stronger peppers we grew, and Han'zir blows furiously as he tries to clear the spice from his tongue.

"You didn't have to burn my mouth," he whines. "There's so much pepper in this!"

"Then you make dinner next time," I grumble. Not that he's wrong. I did go a little overboard, but I have an easy remedy. When Han'zir gets up to clean off our trays, I catch the hem of his pants with my thumb. He stops mid-step as I yank them down, and press myself against his back. His dick is still soft, but when I clench my big hand around it, my troll lets out a groan.

What we're doing is, yeah, a little odd. A troll and an orc shacking up? I know. We're outliers. But I sure love how quickly he hardens up in my grip, how soon I can get him grunting and groaning my name as I stroke him. I turn him around and shove him down into one of the chairs, then kneel in front of him, bringing his thick cock into my mouth.

"Oh, fuck," Han'zir says, but not in the good way. He pushes me off. "Your mouth!" He rubs himself, squinting.

"What's wrong with it?" I demand. On top of all the inconveniences today, now he's objecting to a deep throat?

"You burned me! All that pepper, it..." He trails off. "That shit hurts."

I roll my eyes and get back up. I guess he doesn't want me to suck him off then. But I know somewhere else he can put that cock, somewhere that will bring us together the way I'm always hungering for.

I don't even have to say it, because we've been together long enough that Han'zir can read my mind. He licks his chops, then yanks my own pants down until they're in a pool at my feet.

"Turn around," he barks, and I do as I'm told. I like it when my troll gets bossy. A rare treat, and one that lets me put my guard down for a moment. I watch over us, make sure we have food to eat and coin for supplies, and sometimes it weighs on me—but with Han'zir in control, I can let go.

Once I'm standing in front of the table, he reaches in front of me and wraps his big hand around my length. His fingers are warm to the touch and it sends a shiver straight from my balls to my head. I swell in his palm as he strokes. He squeezes hard in just the places I like, the way only he knows how. I'm already falling forward to put both hands on the table, absorbed in the feel of him, of his familiar hands on my body. Han'zir pumps me harder and faster, then reaches around me to grab the oil off the table. After pouring some into his hand, he runs his fingers down between my ass cheeks. Once he reaches the tight hole between them, he pauses, slathering it around, pressing one finger inside me to open me up for him. A thrill runs through me at the idea of having him inside me again, right where he fits. I grunt and square my legs, and his hand on my cock works even harder. He spreads me open for him, putting in two fingers next, and there's seed dribbling from my cockhead onto the table.

Then he's nudging at my ass, pushing his way into me. My body tightens up all over, resisting him at first, and Han'zir pauses. He runs his hand down my back, as if saying, *relax, you brutish orc,* and I try to let all my worries about running the farm go. He withdraws, slathering his seed and the oil around, then presses in again, deeper and deeper, until he's fully sheathed in me.

"Fuck," he groans, letting my cock fall as he gets absorbed in the moment. He grabs my hips and thrusts again, and again, and this time I stroke myself as he pumps inside of me, moaning and gripping me tight. I can feel the slightest burn from my lips on him, but it only heightens the gloriousness of having him inside me.

We may not be mates, but Han'zir knows me better than I know myself sometimes. He finds his way deep, seeking out the place that will make me explode. He buries his face in my back, his tusks almost piercing my skin. Like this, him buried in me up to the hilt, I can almost reach out and touch his soul—but it's just outside my grasp.

"Fuck, Drazak," my troll moans, pumping harder. "You feel so fucking perfect." Then he strikes me right in my favorite spot, and immediately I'm seizing up and jerking in my own hand, my seed shooting out across the table. Han'zir gasps and then shoves himself as far into me as he can, and there's a burst of color behind my eyes as his cock grows and unleashes inside me. Fuck, how does he always feel so good?

That's the moment I hear the chickens squawking.

"Damn it!" I yank us apart, and Han'zir's juices leak out of me. I pull my pants back on, lace them up, and run out the door while he calls my name.

I'm going to catch them, whoever is stealing my eggs, and hang them out to dry.

CHAPTER 2

ESME

When I wake up abruptly, my heart beating fast and my forehead beaded with sweat, I'm almost certain my wound is getting infected. It's hot and red, and I see stars whenever I brush it against something. I need to wash it and try to clean out the dirt, but when I climb down from my spot up in the hay, the chickens scatter and yell at me.

"Sorry, sorry," I hiss at them. "Keep it down." The last thing I need is to attract attention to myself after taking all those eggs this morning and sucking them down raw.

I can't stay here, I know that. But where else can I go? I'm deep in enemy land with no idea where I am. If I wandered farther, I might come across trollkin soldiers, and then I'd definitely be dead.

There's nowhere in this world for me, not anywhere. I can't even go back home because everyone would know I was a deserter.

I step outside the barn and look around. A trollkin came in earlier today, and I hid carefully behind a big bale of hay up in the loft while he did his chores. He was the green kind, an orc, with a bare chest, a sturdy belly and tree-trunk-thick legs. His tusks looked deadly.

Eventually I'll figure out what to do if I can just survive for now, but I can't be seen by that guy. Perhaps if I'm quiet and clever, I'll find something else to eat before retreating back to my hiding place.

That's when I hear a roar, and the angry stamping of boots.

Shit. He's coming back.

I clamber up the ladder to the hay loft, and slink into the back without making the wood creak. I plant myself behind a hay bale and hold my breath as the orc charges inside the barn, growling some words in Trollkin I can't understand as he hangs up his lamp. He opens a door, checks inside, then slams it in irritation. He scatters the chickens as he searches the nests, then stops.

The ladder. The rungs squeak as he steps on the first one, then the second. I squeeze myself even tighter into the back, hoping he won't see me past the big bale I'm crouched behind.

Another rung and another, and he's standing right at my height. I can see his face from here, and it's...

Not what I expected at all. Far more familiar than illustrations of trollkin had led me to believe, with their monstrous, disgusting faces and huge, deadly tusks. He has a broad nose and thick brows, which are drawn together in annoyance as he searches the loft. Firm lips wrap around his rather short tusks, but they're pulled down in a frown. His dark hair is loose and chopped irregularly, and he pushes some away from his face as he peers into the back, scouring the hay for his intruder.

But his big yellow eyes graze right past me, and he huffs when he doesn't see anything inside. He retreats down the ladder, and I let out the breath I've been holding for the last minute.

At the sound, he shoots up, grabbing the big hay bale in front of me. "*Ag yaz argak!*" He pulls it to one side—revealing me crouched in the very back, trying as hard as I can to make myself small.

"Please," I say, crawling away from his reaching arm. "Please don't hurt me." The orc snarls as he climbs up into the loft and seizes me by the wrist. My arm screams in agony. "No, please!" Tears are streaming down my face as the terror and the pain overtake me. I can't die now, not after how much I went through to get this far. What will they do to me? String me up in the middle of the town square, or chop off my head, or something worse?

The big trollkin drags me begging and crying out of the loft, then tosses me to the ground. I land hard on my back and it throws all the breath from my lungs. My wound tears open, any of the barest healing it might have done gone as I struggle to breathe. Gasping, I curl onto my side and grip my wound tightly to protect it.

A pair of massive boots land next to my head. I try to get back to my feet, but next thing I know, his huge hand has wrapped around my neck. He hauls me up into the air, and my cry catches in my throat where he's crushing my windpipe. I flail, but my legs only meet the unforgiving plane of his belly.

"Please," I choke out, "don't kill me. I'll do whatever you want. Please."

I search his bright yellow eyes, willing him to understand me, begging him with every last ounce of my being to let me go. He glares back, enraged, ready to tear me apart. These are my last moments, I'm sure of it.

Please, I say silently, choking as he tightens his grip. *Don't kill me. I've come too far to die.*

Suddenly, his brows loosen. Then his eyes grow wide and his hand goes slack around my throat. I fall to the ground in a heap, gasping and clawing at my neck, trying to get the breath back in my lungs.

What did I see in there just now? It was like... a flash of recognition, as if somehow, this orc and I have met before.

I gag a few more times, and glance up as he crouches down next to me. I roll away, fully intending to jump to my feet and make a run for it, but he grabs onto me again, holding me in place.

"*Zurek ag yar*," he growls, and I fall still before he can choke me a second time. His hand travels down my arm to my hot wound and I resist the urge to flee with all my power. When he leans forward, I'm afraid he's going to use it to hurt me more—but he's only peering at the ripped-open skin. What is he doing? I don't know why he cares whether I'm injured or not.

The orc lets out an irritated grunt, then releases me. Again I try to get my feet under me, to do everything in my power to escape this place where I'll only find pain and death. This time, he lets me get up, but when I turn to run, he snaps something harsh in Trollkin and yanks me back.

I glare back at him, wiping the tears from my face. "What? I'm sorry I ate your eggs, okay? I am. But I'll make it up to you. I'll do anything you want. I'll—"

He slaps a hand over my mouth and barks something angry. I think he wants me to shut up, so I do. I know how to obey, because it's a well-practiced skill. And maybe if I'm compliant, he won't kill me. All I have to do is live long enough to make a plan.

When he's certain I won't speak again, the orc withdraws his hand and snarls. "*Yerzag ag kar gen.*" As his eyes travel down my body, a more horrible thought enters my mind: What if he wants to use me? What if he plans to abuse me before he kills me? I haven't heard of trollkin doing that before to humans, but—

I hear the tromping of more feet. It can't be. Not another one.

But it is, and this must be the worst day of my life.

This time, it's an aqua-blue trollkin who enters the barn, with blue hair pulled up in a sloppy ponytail. He stops dead when he sees me.

Great. All chances of my being able to get out of this alive have flown out the window.

Han'zir

A human.

So that's who ate all the eggs, is it? This little feather of a thing? She's so small and thin, I could pick her up with one finger.

"Look what you found," I tell Drazak, slapping him on the back. "Where was she?"

"Up in the loft," he answers, never taking his eyes off of her. She's glancing from side to side like a trapped deer. "Hiding in the hay."

"Huh. How about that." I lean over his shoulder and peer down at the little human. Her clothes are ratty and her skin is dirty and bruised, like she's been through hell. Her sleeve is torn and under it is a large, bright red gash. Her messy hair is an ashy brown, and her hazel eyes are huge and bright.

I wonder where she came from and why she's here now.

"What should we do with her?" I ask, leaving my orc's side to circle around her. The woman shrinks back from me, her big eyes going as round as a rabbit's before it runs.

"We turn her in, of course," Drazak says without a second thought. "They'll probably toss her in prison and torture her, or maybe put her in the stocks and cut off her hands..."

That all sounds very unpleasant for such an innocent creature as this one. I arch an eyebrow at him.

"This little human?" I ask. Her wary eye follows me as I finish my circle, never turning her back to me. "What has she done to deserve getting her hands cut off?"

Drazak snorts as if it's the stupidest question of all time. "She's a part of all this nonsense. Look." He flicks the military badge on her chest, and the little thing skitters backwards. "Soldier. Who knows how many of our kind she's killed out there?"

"Conscripted," I point out. "Just like we almost were. Look at her clothes. This isn't what a real soldier wears." Only a few of us were spared from conscription, and growing food for soldiers' rations was an essential enough job that we made it out. Many of our trollkin brothers and sisters have not been so lucky. "I don't think she would hurt a fly, Drazak."

"So what?" He crosses his arms and glares at me. "She's the enemy, Han. It's not up to us to decide what to do with her. We turn her in, let the authorities take care of it, and most importantly, keep our noses clean."

We don't notice until it's too late that the woman has been creeping toward the wall, where she suddenly snatches a rake. Drazak jumps into action, and I'm certain she's going to try to use the damn thing as a weapon, pointless as that would be. But nobody ever said humans were bright.

Before Drazak can grab her, she scurries away and starts raking the ground like her life depends on it. He pauses as she frantically gathers up stray straws of hay and chicken droppings, too baffled by what she's doing to stop her. We both stare as she makes a little pile, then reaches for a pan off the wall and scoops it all in. Carrying the pan, she heads for the door, but I block her way. I can't have her running off now, not when she's acting in such a curious manner.

With a look of annoyance, she gestures for me to step to one side.

"Stop her," Drazak snaps at me, but instead of doing what he asks—he should know better by now than to try to boss me around—I step out of the way and let her past. With a nod of appreciation, she dumps the pan out with the rest of the animal debris. Then she hurries back and picks up the rake again.

"What is she doing?" Drazak asks, his mouth slightly ajar.

"Helping, I think." I study her as she rakes up more filth. "Fascinating behavior, isn't it?"

She pauses in her raking, then leans the handle on the wall and climbs up the ladder to the hay loft. I follow along, hands tucked behind my back, interested to find out what this odd little creature will do next.

She lies down in the hay and, very dramatically, pretends to snore. It's... adorable.

"She wants to sleep here," I call down to Drazak. The woman's eyes open, and she curls up tighter in the hay, laying her claim on it.

"What?" He frowns deeply. "She can't do that. Not in my barn. She's human."

I drop down the ladder, and she follows me. Once on the ground she rakes again, gesturing at it and then at us, trying her hardest to communicate. The little human is offering a trade.

"I think she wants to work." I tilt my head. "She'll do chores if we let her sleep here."

The girl claps her hands in front of her and blinks the widest, saddest, sweetest eyes I've ever seen in my life. For a moment, I'm enraptured by them.

"No," hisses Drazak. "No way."

"Aww, why not?" I lean forward, supporting my hands on my knees while I inspect her closely. The human shrinks back. "You said you wanted a dog, didn't you?"

"You can't be serious." He lets out a moan of anguish and drags his palm down his face, like he's trying to rub the frustration out of his skin.

"When am I not serious?" I ask cheekily. "She can take care of the chickens. Keep away those pesky coyotes."

"We can't be harboring a human!" Drazak lets out an agitated breath. "Plain and simple. What if we got caught?"

I stand back up. "Well, what if we're not caught? Then we get this cute human pet who sleeps in a barn like a goat."

Drazak shakes his head in disbelief. "Cute?"

I gesture at her. "You know. Like a baby fawn. Stupid, weak, endearing." His eyes follow my hand, taking in the demure creature in front of us. "You're considering this," I say, taunting. "You don't want that sweet little neck of hers snapped in half at the gallows, do you?"

With one last displeased snarl, Drazak turns on his heel and stomps out of the barn. I know then that I've won.

I grin down at the human and point at the ladder. "All right," I tell her. "You can stay there." I mime sleeping. "And in exchange, you'll do whatever I tell you. Okay?" I mime sweeping again.

She nods eagerly, the sides of her big mouth pulling up in a smile. It sends a very strange tingle down my spine.

I lead her over to the ladder, and she comes along eagerly behind me. "You go to bed now," I tell her, gesturing at the loft. She nods agreeably and clambers up, disappearing into the hay.

We may have just found ourselves a very good dog.

Esme

They're letting me stay.

The two big trollkin are letting me stay in exchange for... well, I'm not sure. I can't sweep the barn floor forever, but there are plenty of other things I can do if they let me. I can chop wood, cook meals, clean, and everything else I did around the master's home. I'm good at making myself useful, because being useful is how you stay out of harm's way. Even if my wound hasn't healed yet, I can still work.

When the teal-blue troll returns the next morning to summon

me—the one with the friendly, curious eyes—I follow him out of the barn into the fields. He tells me important-sounding things that I can't understand while we pass down rows of vegetables. Leaves slide through his fingers as we walk by, and I get the sense just by watching him that he's connected to these plants, and they reach out to him as if they know him.

He leads me all the way back to the clay house on the far other end of the farm, with its strapped leather roof. It's all very strange to me, this place, how foreign it is while also feeling like somewhere I've been before.

We stop behind the house near what looks like a well. The huge trollkin picks up a bucket, then cranks a handle. Sliding the bucket in the hooks, he gestures for me to take over. So I do, cranking and cranking until the bucket reaches the bottom of the well. I fill it, then crank some more to bring it back up to the top. The troll gives a nod of approval and urges me to follow him.

I take the bucket and do as he says, because this is my ticket out of here. If I can convince these guys to trust me, I can sneak out food a little at a time and build up what supplies I might need to make a getaway. Perhaps if I go back the way I came and head south, maybe I could return to the King's lands and find somewhere safe to hide, somewhere I won't be turned in for desertion. Maybe by then the war will be over, and we'll have either won or lost.

The troll points me to a big trough and mimes dumping the water in, so I obey. Then he leads me back to the well.

Again and again, I fill the bucket and empty it into the tub while the troll watches me. His eyes are a deep orange, almost red, and his tusks are much larger than the orc's. I wonder about them, these two strange trollkin living out here, working the land the way humans do.

The gash in my arm tears open and leaks as I crank and crank, but I need to show him I can do this, that I can be useful. Then maybe they'll let me sleep in the barn and eat their leftovers until I'm well enough that I can leave.

When the big tub is nearly full, the troll finally stops me, shooing off the last bucket of water. I fall to my knees, not realizing how much my muscles ached until right now. I've been operating off of pure rush and now it's catching up to me. The troll isn't paying attention as he works on lighting some logs under the iron tub. Eventually the kindling catches, and a small fire starts.

The door to the house flies open, and the big orc stomps out. When he sees me, his eyes narrow like I'm a farm animal he found defecating on his floor. Then his gaze travels down to where I'm clutching my arm.

"Han'zir!" The orc lets out a roar and charges towards me. I fall back, ready to defend myself no matter how pointless it might be against someone his size.

He's changed his mind. I'm going to die.

CHAPTER 3

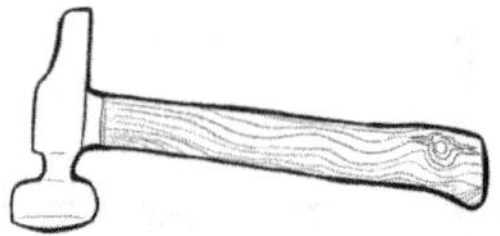

DRAZAK

This idiot. He may be a magician with the crops, but he's useless when it comes to the practical. And now he's worked the damn woman until she's bleeding from that big gash on her arm.

When Han'zir figured out what she was asking of us, what she wanted to trade in exchange for her keep, I shouldn't have stormed out of the barn like I did. But I still can't stop thinking about the way that human *looked* at me. Somehow... I recognized her, like when you see a plate fall and break, and you're certain that same plate has broken before, in that same way but in another time.

In another time, I knew her, whoever she is, and that feeling does not sit well with me.

Then when Han'zir suggested she stay, I liked how that felt even less. The prospect was... enticing. Enticing in a manner that doesn't fit into the order that is our lives, a fantasy that can't work. Things are simple here on the farm, and whatever she is, she promises to be complicated. I heard the sweet lilt in Han'zir's voice as he tried to make an agreement with someone who can't even speak our language. He's immediately taken a liking to her.

This is even less promising. He'll be sorely disappointed when it all goes wrong, and I'll have to pick up the pieces.

As I barge outside to learn what he's been up to for the last hour with his new pet, I find her on the ground, whimpering with pain while dark blood, almost black, drips down her arm. Her face is flushed, her forehead dripping with sweat, and I know just by looking at her she has a fever.

"Han'zir! What have you been doing?" I snarl, rushing towards her. She shrieks and tries to escape, but stopping her takes as much effort as restraining a grasshopper. Holding her captive by her good arm, I peel up her sleeve to get a look at the wound.

Fuck. I should have seen to her injury when we first found her. Now Han'zir has gone and fucked it all up even worse.

"Filling your bath!" he announces proudly, stepping aside to reveal the full, big tub.

"What?" I don't know if I'm hearing him right. "You had the human bring in all the water?" Once more I look down at her bright red face. She's squinting like she expects me to hit her, so I release her good arm, but that doesn't mean I'm done with her yet.

"You're coming with me," I growl at her, and she flinches again.

Han'zir rolls his eyes. "That will certainly make her want to comply," he says, batting me away. He crouches down in front of her, like he's talking to a small child. "Come on. I fucked up, puppy. We have to take you inside." He points at the house, and the woman's eyes follow the direction of his hand. She swallows and nods.

He's a human-whisperer, even when he's the reason she was on the ground in the first place.

Uneasily, she gets up and I lead her into our kitchen, where I dig out some old supplies for bandaging wounds. My skills aren't much, but maybe they'll be enough. If not, I guess she'll probably die. It's not like we can call the village healer to attend to our little human. But that would disappoint Han'zir immensely, since he's already rather attached to his new puppy.

Once she's seated at the table, looking like a child in one of our big chairs, I pull one up next to her to get a good look at her wound. It's angry and red and starting to leak pus.

"This is bad." Again I glare at Han'zir over my shoulder, and he has the sense to look sheepish. "You didn't think at all, did you? About how much work you were making her do?"

"She wanted to prove herself!" He pouts. "I liked it. And I thought you'd enjoy a nice bath."

Of course he did. Not using his head at all, but somehow still sweet about it. I bring over a bowl of water and clean out the wound. The human mewls and pulls back, but I don't relent. There's all sorts of dirt in it. No wonder it's gotten infected.

"Shit," I say with a grimace, and she flinches. I shoot a look at Han'zir. "Go into town. We need something to help your little *puppy* fight this infection."

He nods quickly. "Fine, fine." After shrugging on his pack, he heads out the door. In the meantime, I investigate the bath he had her fill, and find the water already quite warm. Good.

"Come with me," I tell the human, taking her by the wrist. She resists, whimpering like a small animal. Yes, she has every reason to be terrified, but right now I need her obedience—so I lower my voice and urge her on with a gentler command, pointing out the door. "Let's get you cleaned up."

Eventually her suspicion thaws enough that she gets up and follows me outside. I lead her to the tub and indicate she should climb in. Her eyes widen. Some hot water will do her good, and a soak might help the wound, too.

"Get in," I instruct. She hesitates, glancing down at her body and then back up at me.

Great. Modesty. With a grunt of annoyance, I turn around, and then comes the sound of her stripping her clothes off. A tiny voice speaks up behind me.

"Aru haas?" When I look back, she's trying to get into the tub, but it's too high up. Her body isn't curvaceous, but her hips flare out into pert cheeks and her breasts are shockingly large—much bigger than an orcess or trolless in comparison to her tiny shape.

What's even more surprising is how my body reacts to it. I shiver as blood rushes into my hips, and my cock nudges at my pants.

This isn't right. Not at all.

Now I'm irritated. I grab her like I would some chopped wood and heft her into the bath, and her skin is smooth and soft under my hands. The human squeaks when I drop her in the water, then I hastily spin around so I can try to get my infernal dick under control.

I don't understand it. How could I be getting horny for this slip of a human? They're disgusting creatures, and there's nothing in the world I want less than to slide my cock into one. But just the thought makes it jump again, and with a growl I press my hand down on my crotch, trying to will it into submission.

A tiny moan of pleasure undoes all my work. When I turn around, the human has slid down into the water, her hair floating behind her. She submerges her head, and I can make out her breasts once again, and the tight, tiny nipples topping each one like a cherry on a cake. But she's oblivious to me as she floats in the warm water and lets out a sigh of contentment.

I'm overcome by a rush of gratification. This was a good idea on my part. Now she'll be nice and relaxed when I have to inevitably torment her wound later.

I shake my head. I'm already doing her a big favor by seeing to her injuries. I don't need to be worrying about her comfort, too.

I leave her alone in the tub, deciding she's not about to run off —not that she has anywhere to go. It will be some time before

Han'zir returns, so it's not like I can sate my growing need with his body, either. Instead, once I'm inside the house, I take my cock in hand and stroke myself rigorously, pulling the skin back with each stiff pump. I'm so hard it almost hurts. I try to think of Han'zir's tight asshole as I fuck myself with my hand, but my mind keeps drifting back to those tiny nipples, that perky butt. I've had orcesses and even a trolless before, and sucked their soft breasts and spread their wet cunts, but it's never excited me like this.

Something about this human, though, is driving me closer and closer to the edge, and when I shoot my seed, it gets everywhere. There's so much of it that I have to wash the floor before I can call it clean.

I don't want to have to explain that to Han'zir when he gets back.

ESME

When that troll went out of the house earlier, I was afraid of him leaving me alone with his orc friend—or whatever they are. After the way the big green guy treated me in the barn, I was worried something worse might happen. He doesn't seem to like me, that's for sure.

But now he's being so... nice. He put me in a warm bath and then left me alone. I can't wrap my head around it as I lie back in the hot water, relishing how all my muscles relax. Even my arm, which has been pulsing with nail-biting pain ever since he cleaned out the wound, hurts less.

There's a tall stool beside the tub with soap, and rubbing off all the grime and dirt fills me with immense satisfaction. These guys really are living it up out here. They have food everywhere, a clean home, even a bathtub. The biggest one I've ever seen in my life, actually. I could get used to this.

I'm worried about my arm, though, and the orc clearly is, too. I had hoped it would heal on its own, but that's looking less and less likely.

It would be a terrible thing to die when I've just found this place, with these two odd trollkin who have, against all odds, seen fit to take me in. I was told to fear them, to hate them, to kill them. But then I think of Telise and what she said: *They're not what you think they are.*

I'm starting to wonder if she was right.

I don't realize I've fallen asleep until a loud voice rattles me out of my doze. The troll bursts out the back door and rushes over when he sees me, his odd orange eyes alight.

"*Keva,*" he says amiably, sidling up to the tub. He throws out some more Trollkin words I don't understand and offers me his hand.

I think he wants me to get out, but I'm still completely naked and I don't know how I feel about either of them seeing my body. The last thing I want is to give them lecherous thoughts. Do trollkin even see humans that way?

No. That orc doesn't, I know this for certain, not with the way he glared and grouched at me.

Reluctantly, I take the troll's hand and he helps me out of the tub while I cover my breasts with one arm. That doesn't stop his eyes from grazing over me, and one side of his mouth quirks up, bringing his big tusk up his cheek. I turn around the moment I'm out of the bath and reach for my clothes on the ground.

"*Nak zan,*" the troll says sharply, and I halt with my dirty clothes in my arms. He pulls me by the arm, and I use the rags to cover myself as I follow him into the house.

Inside, he brings over a small pile of clothing and sets it on the table. He lifts the first item and flicks his hands to open it up in front of me, revealing a dress made of rusty yellow stitched with beige. It looks much too big for me, but that doesn't come as a surprise given trollkin women are probably a foot or two taller than I am on any given day. He holds it out to me, and only then do I notice the orc standing behind him, arms crossed, with a grumpy scowl on his face. I don't think he likes that the troll brought back new clothes for me.

Tentatively, I take the dress and turn around again as I drop my rags to the floor. It slides on easily, and the fabric is a little crunchy but clean and fresh. It breathes wonderfully, which is a boon in this weather. When I turn back around, the troll claps his hands, saying something to the orc that sounds rather pleased. In response, the orc gives a curt nod. I think he approves.

Crossing my hands in front of me the way I was taught, I bow to them, hoping to show how much this means to me. He went out to buy me clothes—not just one set, but two. And there appear to be other purchases inside a bag over his shoulder.

The orc pats the chair, so I listen and sit down. He's the one in charge, I can tell that much. He snatches the bag and fishes out a few items, one of which is a little glass bottle. He pulls up the sleeve of my new dress, and I know then whatever he's going to do will probably hurt.

Unfortunately, I underestimated exactly how much. I cringe and whimper as he dribbles a few drops in the wound and smears it around. Then he brings out something else, something that turns my blood cold.

A needle and thread.

No. I've seen this done before, when the master's little boy took a big fall and cut the skin of his head open. He screamed bloody murder the whole time he was getting sewn up.

I scramble to flee, but with a growl, the orc grabs me and drags me back down into the chair while he barks instructions at the troll. Grimacing, his companion in torture puts one hand on each of my shoulders and grips me tight, keeping me in place while the orc brings the shining point of the needle down.

I cry out when he spears my flesh, my ragged, angry skin lighting on fire with pain. I squirm and wriggle, trying to escape, but the troll holds me firmly as the needle pierces me, over and over. I'm sobbing by the time he's finished, and he ties off the thread before slicing it with his teeth. A few hiccups escape me, but that's all I have left.

With a sharp nod at me, the orc gets out of his chair to tidy up. The troll crouches down in front of me as I wipe my tears away with my good arm.

"*Yazi keva*," he says, reaching towards my face. I flinch away, but all he's doing is tucking some of my wet hair behind my ear. For a moment, he looks sad, and screws up his lips in a funny way. "*Gro agken.*"

I don't know what the words mean, but it feels like he's apologizing. A troll, apologizing to me? An orc, caring for my wounds? I feel like I've entered another world, and despite the fresh stitches in my arm, I don't think I hate it.

After that the big orc cooks a meal of fresh chicken and roasted vegetables, and I don't know how long it's been since I ate so well. I try to help out, but he pushes me away, and the troll is the one who cleans up at the end of the meal. Even with my bunk arm, I follow him outside so I can do something to help. This is how I'll show that I'm worth keeping around.

"*Keva!*" the troll chastises me. I realize that he's talking to me.

"*Keva?*" I ask. I point at myself. "No, Esme. I'm Esme."

He shakes his head. "*Keva.*" Then he gestures to himself. "Han'zir. *Zak gorkk—*" he points after the orc. "Drazak."

Han'zir and Drazak, is it? I suppose he's decided to call me *keva*, whatever that means. Hmm. I think I like it. Maybe it suits me. I could become someone new here, someone who isn't Esme, maid and deserter.

Han'zir bids me to follow him, and together we go back out to the barn. He gestures at the hay loft and mimes sleeping, giving me another command that ends in *keva*.

He wants me to go to bed? But it's the middle of the afternoon. When I object, though, the troll silences me and points again at the loft. I think he wants me to rest.

I won't object to that. I'm exhausted after Drazak stitched me up, and my face burns from crying. Once I settle myself into the hay, my arm still aching, it's easy to wander off into dreams.

CHAPTER 4

HAN'ZIR

"Go to bed, puppy," I tell her again. Drazak's last command was to make her rest and give her body a chance to heal. We don't know how fast or slow humans recover from injuries, and Drazak told me in no uncertain terms that she couldn't be taxing herself and doing difficult chores if we wanted that arm to stay stitched.

I'm disappointed, of course, because she's so cute and eager to help. She's the type who's pleased when given tasks to do, a caring sort of person who wants to look after everyone else. I can relate to that.

After I've put the human to bed, I saunter back to the house to find where my orc has gone. I feel almost buzzed, a little heat sloshing around in my head. This is all very thrilling. A lot has happened in one day. We've adopted a pet of sorts, and treated a life-threatening wound before it could do too much damage. I've seen a human naked for the first time, which was brilliant and enchanting. I liked the soft planes of her body, all curvy and round.

In our little world, things don't happen this fast. Not much happens at all, actually, which does get old after a while. But I don't think that peace will remain for long with the new puppy around to mix things up.

I'm strangely horny by the time I locate Drazak working on fixing an old wagon. I crouch down behind him and run a hand down his back, pausing to cup his ass when I reach it. He grunts in answer, but doesn't move, so I slide my fingers around to his crotch.

Whoa. He's already hard as a rock. I grin and stroke him over his pants, and he freezes.

"What is it?" he asks, voice hitching ever so slightly.

"I'm not allowed to touch you now?" I ask, devilishly running my hand lower, where I know that soft cockhead is hidden. I squeeze just a tad, and he jerks under me.

"Well, now someone else lives here," he answers in a gruff tone that says this is my fault and I should know it.

"Aw, that doesn't change anything, though." I rub him harder. "Who cares if the puppy catches us fucking?"

I'm surprised when he leans away from me, then abruptly stands. His cock is straining at his pants when he turns around.

"Don't forget that she's a human," he growls to me, and I'm equally as surprised by the fire in his eyes. "A human who is our enemy. Who no one can catch staying here, or they will drag her away and kill her."

Immediately I sober. He's right, and I hate that he's right. Still, it's curious that he's defending the human after getting so grumpy about having her here. But I raise my hands up in the air in surrender and back away. "Then I guess you can fuck me later, like we're some old grandparents. Should I pretend to have a headache, too?"

I can tell by the slight drift of his left tusk upward that he likes the idea of taking me. Before the puppy, he would have done it right now against the wagon.

"There's work to be finished thanks to all the time we lost this morning and this afternoon." Drazak wipes his hands off on his pants and tries to ignore his straining cock. "So you should get to work. And then I'll fuck you so hard after dinner you won't be able to walk."

My whole body shivers. "Is that a promise?" I ask, making sure he gets a good look at my backside as I walk away.

"It's a threat," he answers, and I snort.

But as I head out to the field to get some afternoon work done, I wonder what's really gotten under Drazak's skin.

Esme

I'm having a surprisingly pleasant dream, lying in the yellow grasses that surround the farm, staring up into the sun. There's a light breeze tickling my face, keeping me from getting too warm. For once, things are peaceful. I feel happy, carefree. There is no master, no one shouting *get over here, you cow*. Two tall shadows dwarf me, but I'm not afraid. I close my eyes and they sweep me away.

I wake up to a hand shaking me. It's Han'zir, and his bright orange-red eyes startle me. He's tugging on my arm, saying something in Trollkin I can't understand. He waves for me to come along, so I drag myself out of the nest I've made in the hay and follow him. My arm hurts significantly less now than it did last night, which is a pleasant surprise. I'll have to figure out a way to thank Drazak.

Even before we reach the house I can smell the food cooking. A big fire is roaring in the pit, with two whole chickens roasting over it. Drazak turns them, then sits back down on a log to drink something out of a skin. When he pulls it away, his lips are dark. Some kind of wine, then.

I sit by the fire, keeping to myself so I don't irritate Drazak. He and Han'zir fall into a conversation, quickly forgetting about my presence. I take the moment to watch them while trying to make it look as if I'm actually staring into the fire. They sit on one log together side-by-side, and occasionally Han'zir's hand brushes over Drazak's thigh. It's clear from their body language that they're together.

That answers one question.

When the chickens are done cooking, Drazak carves them and hands out choice pieces of meat. I wait my turn, but then Han'zir gives me a big hunk of his thigh. Drazak chastises him, and for a moment they argue. I wave my hands in the air.

"Don't worry about me!" I say, not wanting to cause a disturbance. But Han'zir shakes the food at me again, and reluctant to offend him, I take it. The roast chicken is perfectly juicy and crisp on the outside, and it tastes amazing going down my throat. Han'zir, pleased with himself, hands me another piece and I take it eagerly. Drazak huffs something under his breath, but doesn't interfere as the troll continues feeding me.

"*Keva grak craggen,*" Han'zir says, nodding in my direction. Right. *Keva.* That's me. The orc mutters something in return, and I wish more than anything I knew what they were saying. Han'zir laughs, and it's a loud, boisterous noise that makes me jump a little the first time I hear it. It brings a wisp of a smile to Drazak's lips.

It takes me a moment to realize that I'm envious. They clearly care about one another, and live a nice, simple life here. Frankly, it seems like bliss. I sigh and stare into the fire, remembering the life I had before the conscription. I spent every day of my waking life looking after the needs of the master and his wife and children, existing in their lives as barely more than a piece of furniture. But these two, for some bizarre reason, have chosen to take care of me. Now they've cooked for me, twice, and I don't like how it feels as if I owe them something.

The master considered the scraps I got from dinner and my dark room in the attic of the house wage enough for my work. No, the real payment I paid for my keep was when he called my name —*come here, bitch*—and used me to vent his anger and frustration. My bruises were how he collected on my debt.

Tomorrow, I decide, I'll make myself useful, as useful as possible. No, I will become invaluable, and perhaps they'll let me stay forever.

After dinner and plenty of the dark liquid that's in the water skin, Drazak and Han'zir are touching more and more of each other. I can take a hint. I get up and wipe off my dress, then head back to the barn.

"*Keva!*" I pause as Han'zir jogs up behind me. He tilts his head and says some words that mean nothing to me.

"Sorry," I say. "I don't understand you."

He frowns pensively, then seems to give up on whatever he was trying to get across. He gives me a pat on the head and ushers me off to bed.

In my hay loft, I can hear Han'zir's cries all the way from the house. I can't help picturing them together, doing whatever it is that would make him scream out that way. A puddle of energy starts in my chest and worms its way down to my hips, where it settles neatly between my legs. I squeeze my thighs together and try to turn my mind away from it, humiliated by the sensation. No, I won't encourage any of that by touching myself the way I want. It's sick and wrong to think of two trollkin with this kind of wishful hunger.

But as the cries echo, and I make out the sound of Drazak

grunting in pleasure, I wriggle with how warm and wet I feel between the legs. I can't help pulling up my dress and sliding my hand under it, finding that sensitive bud hidden between my lower lips. I stroke it a few times as I listen, imagining them in their room, Drazak's big, powerful body thrusting into Han'zir's taller, lankier one. When it gets to be too much, I dive lower, to where my pussy is weeping with my need. I slide one finger in, grinding the heel of my palm into my clit as I pump it inside myself. My head falls back as my bliss takes over, my body rising and falling to the music of their voices off in the house.

I wonder what it would look like—*feel* like—if I were there with them. I'm about to reach the end of the tunnel, light crawling in at the edges of my vision, when I hear a final powerful shout. I moan as my pleasure boils over, and my channel shudders around my hand.

I lie there panting in the silence, feeling like I've done something terrible.

DRAZAK

The next morning, the peculiar little human is already outside and waiting when I step into the pre-dawn. She holds up the basket she's made with the front of her dress, revealing all of her thigh, and happily shows me the chicken eggs she's already gathered up.

Well, there's one less chore to do, and I got a rather pleasant eyeful in the process.

In the house, though, the puppy doesn't surrender them. She arranges the eggs neatly on the table, then takes a pan and sets it over the fire I've built in the pit on the rack. Once it's hot and full of melting butter, she cracks an egg in, then a few more, not once breaking a yolk. I can't help but watch in fascination as she cooks them just long enough that they stop sticking, and then she flicks the whole pan, sending the eggs flying.

I curse out loud, expecting them to all land on the floor. But she catches them in the pan and each one is perfectly flipped onto the other side. She gives me a wide-eyed look because I'm hovering, so I return to my chair.

Han'zir's pleased to find breakfast waiting when he comes down the stairs. "Aw, thanks," he says to me when I hand him a few eggs.

"Don't thank me." I slip one into my mouth, and it's perfectly cooked. "Thank your new puppy."

He turns to her, impressed, and gestures at the food.

"Thank you, puppy," he says. She tilts her head.

"Thank you?" she asks, repeating the words back to us.

"No, no," says Han'zir, chuckling. "You say, 'you're welcome.'"

He repeats it a few times, and she gets the message, then practices it back.

"So we're teaching her to talk now?" I ask him as the human sets about cleaning up.

"Why not? It would make things a lot easier. Then you could tell her what to do."

I suppose that's true, but it feels traitorous to be teaching a human how to speak our tongue.

When she steps outside, ostensibly to get some fresh water for cleaning, I gesture for Han'zir to follow her. "You get the water this time," I snap. "If I have to stitch her up again, you're sleeping outside tonight."

"Yeah, yeah." He bats a hand at me. "I will."

The rest of the day, the human does everything she can to be useful. Some of the crops are ready for harvest, and she watches carefully as we pull up carrots, check them for bugs, and sort them into baskets by size. Then she joins us at the end of the line—next to Han'zir, I notice, and not me, which sends a surprising shock of jealousy through me.

Of course she likes him more. He's kinder to her than I am, and significantly more personable. But what am I supposed to do? She's human. She's the enemy. She's small and weak and disgusting, with perfectly round buttocks, and perfect globes for breasts, and—

Fuck. I'm getting chubby again just thinking about her naked. I turn my eyes back to our work, and I don't think Han'zir is any the wiser as he inspects the vegetables, then carries some off to be rinsed.

Why the fuck can't I stop thinking like this?

Now it's just her and me again, and that feels both thrilling and dangerous. But she keeps her eyes on her work, only occasionally glancing over at me. I sigh, trying to think of how I could convince her I'm not what she thinks I am. I don't want her to be afraid of me the way she is now.

"You're being a really good puppy," I tell her, and she glances up at the word. "I can see that you're trying hard." I force a smile onto my face, but it must look more like a grimace because she shrinks back. I sigh and return to my work, wishing I had even an ounce of my troll's sweetness. But I'm all rough edges and sharp corners.

One thing she does seem to understand is that I'm the taskmaster. She follows me around at a safe distance, watching each job I do and then imitating it as best she can. It's obvious that Han'zir is a bit of a laze-about as he wanders off to the river to take a bath while we work. But she's so focused on me, on getting each step right, that she doesn't even notice him leave.

It feels more than good to be the center of her attention.

I don't want her to strain her arm, though, so when I get to chopping wood, I send her away to go find Han'zir. She understands the message, and looking a little cowed, leaves to search for him.

I chop log after log, thinking about her face each time she smiles at him, and growl to myself. Whatever this feeling is, I don't like it. I chop another log, more forcefully, and hope Han'zir hasn't dropped a beehive into our lives by taking her in.

CHAPTER 5

Esme

I wish I knew what I needed to do for the orc to like me. Drazak is severe, to say the least. His brows are always furrowed, and when he talks, it comes out a bark or a growl, like a mean dog.

But I'll take severity over my master's fake sincerity. He always put on a smile for guests and family, but I knew all his tells, when he was about to come unhinged and I would become his convenient target. I could sense the mood in the house change as he filled with fury, and I learned how to run before he could make me his punching bag. I'm smaller and faster, and even when he chased me, I learned quickly how to outrun him.

No, Drazak is all bark and no bite. I try my hardest to impress him anyway, because more than anything, I want his approval. When I do something right and he gives me a gruff nod, I feel like I've won a prize. I only wish that I knew what it took to make him smile.

I think I would like the way Drazak smiles if he were smiling at me.

Han'zir is far more free with his affection. He teaches me words for things, like how to say *chicken* in Trollkin, or *cow*, or *horse*. I learn all the polite words like *hello, goodbye, please*, and *thank you*. I'm picking up what the vegetables are called, how to announce that dinner is ready, and what I need around the farm to do my chores. I try to make the meals whenever possible, and I think my cooking impresses them because Han'zir and Drazak always make pleased little noises as they eat. Once I discovered the herb garden and the pepper plants, Drazak stopped trying to fight with me over who was going to use the pan that night.

One thing I've learned is that Han'zir has nothing in the way of modesty. Often, he goes and bathes in the river alone, but every so often he warms up the bathtub and gets in it, sighing with pleasure as he slips down under the warm surface of the water. I'm heading back to the house with vegetables for dinner when I catch him getting out, completely naked, his wild blue hair soaked through and lying flat down his back.

There's muscle. A lot of it. It frames his big chest, his powerful abdomen, trailing all the way down to his groin and thighs. That's when I tear my eyes away, though I did catch a glimpse of what was between his legs.

In relation to his body, his cock is a normal size. But compared to me... I hold up my hands like a pair of blinders and bolt inside, almost slipping on the steps in my hurry. Han'zir's chortle follows behind me. I slam the door and lean against it, my breath suddenly coming short and fast. I feel like I've run a marathon.

Why did the sight of that stir a sudden, primal need in me? I shake my head, trying to clear the image from my mind, but it's lodged there now. I think of his cries coming from the house, and the heat running through my blood threatens to catch fire.

When I glance up, Drazak is staring at me, and for once his brow isn't deeply creased. I'm idling, and I don't want to idle in front of him. That was always the master's rule: the help—me and Benny, the butler—must always look busy. The only time I could rest was when everyone else was asleep. Then I'd take a breather, maybe read a book. Usually, I was so tired I passed out with the pages smooshed against my face, wasting a candle when I was only allowed one a month.

So while Drazak watches me I set about tidying, as much as you can tidy a house that's already clean. I neaten the wood pile and clear the table, trying my hardest not to think about what I saw, or imagine what it looks like when Han'zir and Drazak are naked in their bedroom. I chew on my fingernails as I debate what else I can do to appear busy.

"*Keva.*" Drazak's voice is as gruff as always. I spin around, clasping my hands behind my back. My arm doesn't hurt at all now. I have to thank him for that when I figure out how.

"Yes?" I ask in Trollkin, appearing attentive.

The line that travels down his stern, wide-jawed face deepens. I think I've displeased him somehow.

He gestures at the floor next to him at the fire and says a word that's familiar. I think he wants me to sit down. Doing as I'm told, I kneel on the floor a polite few feet away. With a grunt of annoyance, Drazak urges me closer to him, and I wonder what it is he wants. Will he show me something, perhaps a spot I missed when I was cleaning?

Once I scoot over, though, he doesn't say anything else and turns back to the fire. I wait and wait for him to tell me what to do, but nothing comes. Eventually I shift to a cross-legged position, staring into the flicking flames along with him. I can pick up his scent from here, earthy and the tiniest bit greasy from working on farm equipment. He smells strong and hardy, like not even a mountain could knock him over.

I wonder what the purpose of this was? Sitting next to him

quietly, though unsettling at first, eventually becomes comfortable. For the first time Drazak seems relaxed, as much as he does when Han'zir enters a room. He might act a little harsh, but the soft spot he has for the troll is obvious. I find that I envy it, how Drazak smiles when Han'zir gets sassy, which is often. I wish that maybe, just maybe, he would look at me like that, too.

But attention is never good. Standing out means a stick to the knees from the major, or a harsh reprimand from the master. It's much better to go unnoticed, to pass from one task to the next like a ghost.

Still, I shuffle a hair's breadth closer to Drazak, finding I want even more of that musky smell that reminds me of the farm, of sunny days caring for the crops, of *home*. His gaze drifts down to mine, and for the first time, he doesn't seem angry with me. I like how it looks on him, how the lines of his face smooth out, how handsome it makes him look.

I hope he hasn't heard my thoughts, but he tilts his head towards me like maybe he has. He's just begun saying, *"Keva..."* when the door flies open.

Han'zir has managed to dress himself, and when he joins us by the fire, Drazak draws away from me, clearing his throat and getting up as he finds some excuse to busy about. Han'zir glances between us, one eyebrow raised.

I wish that I could have heard what Drazak was going to tell me. When I fall asleep that night in my loft, I imagine many different soft words that might have come out.

HAN'ZIR

There is something peculiar going on between Drazak and the puppy. I don't quite know what it is yet, but believe me, I'm watching with fervent interest. My mother said I've always had a sense of things, a knowing beyond what we can see. And right now I am certain there is a wire strung tight between them, taut and waiting to be plucked.

She is fascinating, the little human. I admire how hard she works for Drazak's approval. I encourage her whenever possible to draw his attention, to get closer to him, hoping maybe she'll break through one of his high, thick walls. He could use that, I think. It's not good for him to be so tense all the time.

That's the other interesting thing. My orc has become far more self-conscious, and works even harder than before. When Esme is around, his muscles clench like he's trying not to break something. It's curious, because I don't think he hates her. He's snappish and huffy sometimes, but never cruel. He doesn't even raise his voice with her the way he does with me. But he's always so stiff that I wonder if it gives him some uncomfortable strain.

To top it all off, Drazak's sex drive has gone through the roof. I didn't mind it at first, but now I puzzle over what it means. Does he feel this hunger for her, too?

One night, while he's buried inside me up to the hilt, searching around for his prize while he slowly strokes my cock, we hear a scream from the barn.

Esme.

Immediately Drazak is moving, leaving me on my hands and knees on the bed. He snatches his pants up off the floor and yanks them on while he blazes out of the house.

I'm not far behind as we race towards the barn. Another of Esme's shrieks echoes across the field. She's yelling something in her language, angry and frantic.

When we reach the barn, she's got a rake in her hand, and she's surrounded on three sides by coyotes. There's an injured chicken on the ground and she's standing over it, rake raised and ready to attack.

"Puppy!" I call out. The moment they see us, the coyotes scatter. A human woman, maybe they could have taken her. Two full sized trollkin? Absolutely not.

When we approach, Esme falls to her knees next to the chicken. "I'm sorry," she says, trying to help it back to its feet. But it's not going to survive. Her eyes are red. "I'm sorry." She looks more panicked at the idea that we'll be angry at her than the fact she was almost attacked.

"Hey," I say, reaching out to touch her shoulder. She flinches at first, but relaxes into me as I rub a circle on her back. "This wasn't your fault." I shoot a sidelong glance at Drazak. "You did your best to protect it."

He doesn't react at first, his eyes simply wide and his breathing ragged. Then, with an imperious sureness in his steps, Drazak marches over and picks up the chicken. He snaps its neck in one short, quick movement, and the creature falls dead. Esme gasps, covering her mouth as he stalks out of the barn, not waiting for us to catch up.

We follow along behind him, and I don't think either of us know what he's up to.

First, he starts the fire pit and strips the chicken. He spears it through and sets it over the flames before retreating into the house. When he comes back, he carries two separate flasks, and puts one in each of our hands.

Esme stares down at hers blankly, then up at him again with a question in her eyes.

"Drink," he urges, in that same harsh tone that he seems to purely reserve for her. When I give him a searching look, he shrugs his shoulders defensively. "What? It will help calm her nerves."

So he's worried about her nerves, now?

Tentatively she takes a drink, and her eyes grow huge. Berry wine has that effect, which is what makes it quite dangerous. I wonder if Drazak knows what he's doing. She takes another big sip, and the tight curl of her shoulders, the shivering in her arms, begins to ebb. After a third sip, I take the skin away from her.

"She shouldn't drink *too* much," I say. Esme reaches for the wine skin in my hands.

"Han'zir," she grumps. "I want to drink that."

"Wow." I grin at her. "Guess your Trollkin is coming along." I'm too proud of her for figuring out how to say what she wants to keep the wine away from her. She happily takes it back.

"She's no better than a toddler," Drazak says. He borrows my skin and guzzles the wine down, too.

And that's when I realize it. He was scared. He ran out there like the barn had caught fire, maybe faster than I've ever seen him move. I take the drink again from Esme and suck down a few big sips myself. I feel like my heart has only just stopped trying to escape my chest. I was terrified of what might happen to her out there, all alone in the barn.

I watch the little human as the meal cooks and the fire reflects off her big eyes.

"What if those coyotes had gotten her?" I ask Drazak.

He flinches. "What? They wouldn't have. They just thought they could force her to back down." But I'm not sure if he believes his own words.

"Drazak—" I begin.

He raises a hand to stop me. "I know what you're going to say, and the answer is 'no.' She is not sleeping in the house. The barn was enough of a stretch."

"But she's not safe out there!" Our burgeoning argument has attracted Esme's attention, and she watches us curiously with the wineskin in her hand.

"So what?" Drazak spits on the ground. "She's a puppy, remember? Dogs don't sleep in the house."

Why is he being so obstinate now when he was the one who

ran like a bolt of lightning to rescue her? When he started this fire and cooked up the dead chicken to make her feel better?

A flame of anger sprouts in my chest. It's not a common feeling for me, but I can't stand the idea of finding Esme lying in a pool of her own blood just because she tried to protect the chickens again.

"She is not a dog," I snap.

"Is that right?" Drazak doesn't rise to my bait, simply arching an eyebrow at me. "I thought she was your pet. And pets live in the barn."

The fire in me burns higher. "You know she's more than that." How could he say that after all she's done around the farm? How hard she works every day to please him, when I wish it were *me* she was trying so hard to impress?

"Hmm," is all Drazak says, taking a sip of berry wine. "No, I don't know that."

He's lying to me—bottling up how he really feels and pretending like it doesn't exist at all. I get up from the log and cross my arms, glaring down at him. "How can you be such a bastard?"

"Because she's just a human!" He rises to his feet, too, and gets right in my face. "You know that, I know that. This can't be permanent. She's a passing fancy of yours, and I've entertained it to make you happy."

My heart clenches. A passing fancy? My eyes slide over to where Esme is watching us both, her face slack in surprise. I hope she can't understand what he's saying about her.

"She's not," I say, but it comes out less strong. Maybe he's right. Maybe this twinge of excitement I feel when she smiles at me, the way my blood feels too hot when I catch sight of her naked backside, will waft past like a cloud across the sky.

"You plan to keep her?" Drazak says, tone accusatory. "To let her sleep at the foot of the bed?"

"I…" I trail off. Of course I want her to stay here, by our sides. I want to keep teaching her how to talk so I can find out what else is inside her mind. I want to watch her finally break through to Drazak, to unlock the affection towards her that he's clearly holding tight inside and refuses to act on. "Why not?" I finally ask. "What harm does it do to keep her? She's helpful. If she wants to stay here forever, then—"

"Since when has 'forever' been on your timeline?" Drazak asks, his face as hard as stone.

It slices me straight through. This is a very old argument, a wound I thought had healed over.

We've never made pledges to each other, Drazak and I. Once he asked me if we might make our bond a lifelong commitment. Though what I feel for him is unparalleled, while my need for his smiles and his body are all-consuming, it's not a mate bond. I know it and so does he. While that doesn't make a difference for him, since he's long given up on such a thing... sometimes I still wonder if it's out there for me. A mate is what I've wanted all my life, and I couldn't pledge myself to Drazak if I was meant for another.

So out of fear, I refused his heartfelt request.

Drazak didn't speak to me for a week. Just when I thought I might crumble and agree to making the pledge, if only to have him back, the cloud abruptly passed and he returned to normal. My relief had been a tidal wave. He wouldn't demand it after all. We could continue our lives as before.

But now it's clear he's not forgiven me, not at all. The stitches have popped out and the wound is bleeding again.

"I..." My thoughts have slowed to molasses as I realize I'm now standing in the center of a room full of mousetraps. "Drazak..."

He just shakes his head, then turns around and stalks away, leaving me standing by the fire with the wineskin in hand.

I sit down on the log next to Esme, whose mouth is round as she watches Drazak leave us. Her eyes travel to me, and there's pity in them. Maybe she can't understand everything we're saying, but it must be clear enough what happened.

I drove him away. I've hurt him, deeply. But it hurts me, too, that he refuses to see what's right in front of us. That Esme is a part of our family, who shouldn't be sleeping in the barn for bears or wolves to find.

She scoots towards me and puts a tiny, gentle hand on my shoulder. I lean into it because with the wine in my blood and my fire extinguished, all I want is comfort. Her little arm reaches around my back and she rubs in soothing circles there, the way I did for her. When I lower my head to rest on hers, I breathe her in and find it's a sweet, almost fruity scent, though a little dusty from sleeping in the barn. It's so reassuring that I bury my face in her hair and find myself pulling her closer.

I hold her like that, taking my selfish comfort in her, until the flames of the fire die down. When true darkness has fallen, Esme disentangles herself and gets to her feet, brushing off her dress. I don't like how cold I feel without her, so I get up, too.

"Good night," she tells me in her adorable, terrible accent, and starts off towards the barn to go to bed. But I follow along behind, and she quirks an eyebrow at me.

"Go on," I say, and her eyebrows rise. Then with a nod, she continues back to the hay loft. Drazak won't want me in our bed anyway, not if he's as angry as I think he is.

Besides, I can't leave her unprotected again, not after tonight.

I climb up the ladder behind her, getting a good look under her dress. The creamy expanse of her thigh sends a sharp burst of need straight down to my groin.

That's just great. First Drazak kicks me out, and now the wine is making me horny for a human. I shake my head as she finds her place in her nest. This is only a result of my unspent need after Drazak and I were interrupted earlier.

I crawl into the hay next to Esme, holding in all the boiling hurt

I feel. She quietly inches towards me and peers into my eyes, giving me a look of deep sympathy as she says, "I'm sorry, Han'zir." She may not know what Drazak and I were fighting about, but she knows I need her. I draw her into my arms and crush her against my chest, where she stays, running her hand up and down my chest.

Maybe it isn't fair to her to use her this way, but then again, maybe Drazak is right. She is just a pet, after all.

CHAPTER 6

Drazak

I didn't mean to bring it up, but I couldn't stop myself. I thought I'd forgiven him, that it was good enough for me to have Han'zir beside me at all.

We share a home and a life, but still he couldn't make a commitment to me. Now he wants to share everything with some human who showed up out of the blue?

I'm glad Esme can't understand us. How would she feel knowing that Han'zir only sees her as a toy, an object to be kept and petted until he stops being amused by her? The sting of it grows even sharper teeth when Han'zir doesn't return to the house. My mind conjures all sorts of terrible thoughts the longer his side of the bed remains empty. He was addled with wine earlier, and I left him and Esme alone.

But there are no telltale sounds, no sign that anything untoward is happening out in the barn. Perhaps he's trying to respect me by not coming to bed, though that's the last thing I wanted.

Still, I imagine Han'zir on top of her, his cock sliding in and out of her, and I have to shut my eyes hard to keep the invasive thought away. Is it that I hate the idea of him enjoying her? Or is it the image of him doing it without me?

Eventually I fall asleep into a tangled web of dreams. In each one, the human is at the center of the storm, all of our eyes turning to her as if she is the one bright spot in the night.

The next morning I awake to find Han'zir and Esme both already up and making themselves useful. Esme's cooking while Han'zir cleans up the remains of last night's meal. He jerks upright when I step out the front door, pain clearly written across his face.

"Drazak—" he begins, taking a few steps towards me. I raise a hand flat, and he halts.

"You slept with the human?" I ask.

His eyes go wide. "I mean, I slept next to her, but nothing else happened." He pauses, then his mouth creases in a smirk. "Are you jealous?"

"What, jealous that you were out in the barn all night?" I scoff, but I'm relieved to hear he kept his hands to himself. He has a hungry cock, too, and part of me did fear the worst—probably because if it were me, I wouldn't have had so much self-control. "I'm not jealous of that in the least."

Han'zir sighs with relief, and then glancing around to make sure we're not being watched, he closes the distance between us. He seizes my face in his hands and drags me in for a kiss, and as much as I want to resist it—to punish him for the hurt that still festers just under the surface—I can't. His mouth hungrily tastes mine and I let him in. Then I turn it around on him, bruising his lips in my quest to reassert my ownership of him. He groans underneath me, and I can't stop my hands from venturing around his body, squeezing his tight ass, rubbing over his crotch. He thickens up under my hand and I'm gratified I can turn him on so easily.

I pull away, leaving him dazed, and get on with my chores.

Now I have two dogs at my feet while I'm busying around the farm, trying to make themselves useful. Esme is a little more competent, though, so eventually I turn to Han'zir and snap at him to find something else to do. There's plenty of planting to finish, his specialty, and I don't want to keep thinking about our argument last night. I want to pretend it never happened and continue life as usual.

Not that life will ever be usual again with Esme around.

She helps me sow seeds, and unless I'm imagining it, she keeps less of a distance than before. Her brown eyes jump to me often, as if checking on me, monitoring my mood. I enjoy her quiet companionship, how she stays close by my side as if I'm her protector. When she bends over, my eyes are drawn to her small rear, to the thighs that poke out when she hikes up her dress to kneel, all the way to her tiny feet in her ratty shoes.

We should probably replace those, but I don't know anyone who sells boots that small. I might have to make them myself.

After our argument, there is no more talk of bringing Esme inside the house. Every night as we go to bed, I worry about her alone in the barn, what would happen if a bear or a wolf came looking for a meal. But I say nothing. It's just a risk we have to take to keep my hunger at bay.

When she drops a bowl and it clatters on the ground, she hastily picks it up and cleans the mess she's made. "She's so cute," Han'zir says as he helps her. It grates on me when he talks about her like she's a kitten to be admired for its little claws, how he pats her on the head the way one would a real dog. Can't he see that she is a woman, with a smooth, soft body waiting to be caressed?

I try to banish these thoughts, but no matter what I do, they worm their way back in.

Esme

I still don't know what to make of their argument over the fire. Drazak had been angry, yes. But whatever was said... he was hurt, too, and so was Han'zir. Shame bites at me because in the middle of it, I heard *keva*, and I was certain that the argument was somehow about me.

I thought about leaving after that. I've assembled a decent store of food in the hayloft in the very back, some of which has already started to go bad. By now I should've left already, but the truth is that I like it here. Drazak and Han'zir have nothing in common with my master back home, who would twist my arm behind my back and mutter horrendous things in my ear when I didn't do a task exactly to his specifications. If I mess up on the farm, Drazak rolls his eyes and takes over, shooing me to go do something else. They don't hit me, or even boss me around. They value my work, Han'zir praising me when I do a job well, or Drazak offering a curt nod. They let me eat with them instead of in a separate room where I can't be seen. They treat me like I'm one of them, a member of their family, even though I still sleep in the barn.

That was the trade, after all, and as long as they let me stay, I'll abide by it happily.

I am happy, I realize. I know the roles and the rules here, and that certainty fills me with a contentment I haven't had before. So the last thing I want is for Drazak and Han'zir to be fighting over me—but I fear leaving the one home that's ever made me feel worthy.

What else is out there but pain and rejection? To be treated as no better than a farm animal, a thing to be used as a vessel for my master's fury?

At least here, I'm safe from the war. Here, no one knows I'm a deserter. The battle is happening far away.

Or so I thought, until the horses come thundering down the road.

Drazak and I are deep in our work, scattering chicken droppings in the soil to restore the nutrients it lost in the harvest. We have it down to a system, where he pulls the cart and I shovel, and then we'll pass over it again with the tiller to mix it all together. Later, Han'zir and I will plant the seeds, because he knows exactly how far to space them and how deep to bury them to ensure they thrive.

But our peace is shattered when a dozen horses approach the house, carrying trollkin in various shades of green and blue—all of them armed.

"Fuck!" Drazak growls. I let out a squeak of surprise as he grabs me around the middle. Tucking me under his arm like a sack of carrots, he takes off at a sprint towards the house, where Han'zir stands at the back door, fear twisting his usually amiable face. I try to ask him what's going on, but Drazak claps a hand over my mouth so I can't make a sound.

The horses come to a halt outside as I'm carried into the bedroom, and there, I'm unceremoniously tossed onto the bed.

"Quiet," Drazak says in his most commanding voice. There's no time for explanation before he turns and slams the door.

Those horses must mean something very bad, so I keep silent like he instructed. I crawl under the bed to hide, though I can still hear Han'zir and Drazak's panicked whispers. Whatever is happening, they're terrified. An ominous air fills the house, and then there comes a loud, heavy knocking at the door.

Are they here for me? Did someone see me here, living and working on the farm, and now they've come to collect?

The floor under the bed is covered in dust, and I do my best not to sneeze. Outside the bedroom, the front door opens and boots tromp inside. I can make out the sound of a stern, raised voice, but I can't understand any of the words. I squeeze myself even tighter against the wall, hoping against hope they don't find me and take me away.

I don't want to leave my troll and my orc. I don't want to die after finding peace and happiness for the first time in my life.

Drazak barks something in return, and it escalates into loud arguing. He's exactly the type who won't back down from a fight, and worry pools in my belly. What if they hurt him to get what they want? I beg him silently to stay calm, to let them take and do what they want, even if that thing is me.

I can't let something happen to him. Maybe I should walk out of this room and turn myself in, so they won't get hurt.

But my cowardice, the sense of self-preservation that sent me fleeing from the war in the first place, keeps me trapped under the bed.

Han'zir

The big, beefy troll is dressed in a dirty uniform, a whole troop of soldiers and wagons waiting on the road behind him.

"It's for the war effort," he says, without any give in his deep baritone. "Now let us in."

At least they're not here for *her*. Would I let them drag her away if it meant we might come out unscathed?

No. Of course not. And that certainty frightens me in more ways than one.

"We need that food to survive!" Drazak snaps, blocking his way into the house.

"Drazak," I hiss, holding him back by the arm. "Let them take it." The last thing I want is for the soldiers to decide he's putting up too much of a fuss and spear him through to get him out of the way.

"No!" He shoves me off. "We won't make it through winter without that food."

"The fight against the humans requires sacrifice from all of us," the troll says, taking a step closer. He's taller than Drazak, but that doesn't stop my orc from getting in his face.

"We can't keep raising rations if we're starving," Drazak snarls. "What will you feed the troops then?"

"That's not my concern." The troll crosses his arms and glares down. "I'm here on behalf of the Grand Chieftain, and these are my orders. If you don't step aside, there will be consequences."

"Try me," Drazak says, his shoulders curling. He's ready to fight. But before I can intervene, the troll socks him right in the face.

Drazak stumbles back, clutching his nose. He raises his own fist to strike, but if he attacks an officer, he'll certainly pay the price.

"Drazak!" I'm firm this time when I yank him to the side. I'm taller and stronger, and right now, I'm going to assert it. "We can't stop them." My eyes slide to the bedroom door, where our little puppy is hiding. The more Drazak puts up a fight, the more suspicious they'll be that we're hiding something—that we're stowing away food for ourselves. If they search the house for leftovers, they'll find Esme and most certainly kill her.

This thought drives a stake through my belly.

Drazak follows my eyes, and finally, catches my meaning. Bleeding from his nose, he steps aside to let the soldiers in with a grim, defeated look.

First, they take everything they can find in the kitchen, rooting through barrels of smoked meat and vegetables to find what's inside, and rolling them out the front door to load into the wagons.

They even take the butter Esme churned yesterday, and all the milk from our ice chest. More soldiers file through the house and out the back door, toward the fields—and our livelihood.

We watch from the back step in silence as they fan out across the farm, stripping the plants bare, even ones that haven't reached maturity. What will some unripe corn do for them? Nothing. They want to hurt, to torment, to take, and we are a convenient outlet for their rage.

When they reach the barn, we hear the chickens squawking wildly, then the *shhk!* of blades coming down, silencing their cries one after another. More soldiers ride out into the pasture, rounding up the cattle only to butcher them one by one. Then they drag the corpses out to their wagons, loading up piles of headless cows and chickens. When they find the storage shed, it's a free-for-all, and the rest of the wagons are filled with produce, grain and anything else they could scrounge up.

Neither of us move, or even speak, as they rip away everything we have.

Hours later, when they've finished their rape of our fields and our livestock, the soldiers climb back on their horses and thunder away with their wagons full of loot, taking our entire life's work with them.

I'm surprised when Drazak sinks to his knees on the ground, covering his face with his hands. His whole body trembles, and I crouch down beside him, pulling him into my arms. He shudders against me, his face hot and wet, and all I can do is hold him as our future burns to ash.

When I free Esme from the bedroom, I don't expect her to hurl herself against me, wrapping her arms around my waist. Her face is bright red from tears, and she rubs it against my chest, saying my name over and over. When Drazak steps in the door, she disentangles herself and rushes over to him, checking his bloody nose and wiping it with her dress. He's surprised by such close attention

—even more so when she hugs him for all he's worth. His gaze travels to mine as he wraps his arms around her in return. Then he sinks into her, his eyes squeezing closed to hold back tears. She kisses his forehead and soaks up as much of his pain as she can, but the well is bottomless.

We've lost everything.

Chapter 7

Esme

They came. They took. They left. In their wake is one broken orc and one troll trying very hard to stand up straight. I do my best to help, even if that just means holding Drazak tight.

They saved me. Not just from the war, not just from starvation, but from those soldiers, too. They hid me when they could have turned me in, when maybe it would have helped them.

I think of Telise then, and what she said to me. *See, little maid, it's just a matter of perspective.* This war has taken just as much from them as it's taken from us. I was thrown onto the front lines with nothing but my axe. They've had their livelihoods stripped away.

At least the soldiers didn't take the seeds. While Drazak sits on a log, staring into nothing, I get to work. I till some soil, which was disturbed when the invaders ripped out all the tiny onions just starting to grow, and then set to planting. After a while, Han'zir joins me.

"Thank you, *keva*," he says to me, bumping his shoulder against mine. He forces a smile.

I just shake my head. This is the very least I can do.

In the late afternoon, I tell them I'm going out. I gesture off towards the trees, where once upon a time I looked down on this valley and saw my salvation.

"What?" Han'zir frowns at me. "Alone? That's not a good idea."

I nod with enthusiasm. I can go alone. It's not far, and I won't be seen. "It's all right," I tell him. "I'll be fine."

For the first time in hours, Drazak raises his head. I've never seen him look quite so... defeated. Every muscle in his face is slack, his eyes are red, and his hands are trembling. He shakes his head at me.

"Don't go," he says, and all of his usual gruffness is gone. I want to throw my arms around him again, to bring him even some small ounce of comfort, but I don't know if he would welcome it.

"I'm going," I say, standing firm. I know what I need to do. I grab two baskets, one in each arm, and set off. If the soldiers find me, they find me, but I can't let my trollkin go hungry tonight.

I search high and low for berry bushes, scrounging for the nuts that sometimes grow on trees, and gather everything I can. There are edible greens, too, and if I'm really enterprising tomorrow, maybe I can catch a rabbit or a quail. Something to feed the hungry bellies that are sure to come.

Han'zir gets to his feet when I return, taking both baskets from me. As he pets my head, there's a sincere fondness in his eyes.

We eat the few apples, berries, and nuts I found, sharing them amongst ourselves. I take as little as possible, but after a while Drazak firmly sets down an apple in front of me. When I open my mouth to object, he gives me a death glare, so I shut it and take the offering.

That night, the barn is quiet and lonely without the chickens I've gotten so accustomed to living with. There's one single egg left in a nest that they didn't take. I'll make sure to cook it for Drazak in the morning.

Maybe that can be one small joy in the middle of all this mess.

The next day, the orc tries to put on a pleased face for me when I serve the egg to him, but it's only on the surface. I didn't think I would ever miss the growly Drazak I've come to know, but seeing him this way, with no fighting spirit at all, hurts in a place that's new and tender. When I take his plate away, I pause to hold his hand in mine—getting my fingers around just two of his big ones—and grasp them firmly. I want him to know I'm here.

Han'zir stops on his way past and leans down to kiss him, and Drazak's eyes fall closed. I turn away, not wanting to interrupt their moment, but the troll finds his way to me next. To my immense surprise, he kisses my head, too.

"Good *keva*," he says, nodding toward the egg, then continues on his way, leaving me wondering what he's thinking. Drazak doesn't miss any of it, and his eyebrows furrow like it doesn't make sense to him, either.

DRAZAK

The way little Esme held me, you would think she was much bigger, much taller, much sturdier than the waif she is. She lent me what strength she had, and it was enough to convince me of one thing: It's up to me to make sure we get through this, that all three of us survive.

It is the three of us now, living here on our savaged farm—no more two of us and one dog. Esme has done everything she can to find food, but I'm afraid of her venturing farther afield and running across other trollkin. If something happened to her out there, I'd never forgive myself.

I only manage to land two squirrels the first day I go hunting, but thankfully I have more success the next time. I manage to bring down a small boar, just a young one, but it will feed us for a while. I brought rope along with me, so I tie its legs together, loop the rope around my waist, and drag my prey one slow step at a time back home.

It's late at night when I finally return and gut the boar's carcass on the work table, then hang it up to finish butchering in the morning. I find Han'zir and Esme inside, asleep in front of the fireplace, which has burned down to embers. Esme is tipped over, her head laying in Han'zir's lap, while he's fallen onto his back and now snores peacefully. I study them together, and a tiny warmth flickers in my chest.

Does he still only see her as a thing, as a pet? Or has he, too, felt what I have? But I can't think of a way to talk with him about it that doesn't give away my own need, my own burning lust, for someone that isn't him. I can't do that.

I consider waking them and taking Han'zir back to bed, but then Esme would return to the barn to sleep in the hay, and tonight, I don't want that for her.

I only objected to her living in the house because I feared what having her so close might do to me. Now, as she becomes an even more fundamental part of our lives, as her encouraging smiles and small, hardworking hands buoy my spirit, I'm more afraid of her than ever. There's a pull between us, something I've only ever experienced with Han'zir. It was the reason I chose him when he came doggedly hitting on me at the market.

So I leave them be, considering for a moment that it's selfish of me to make her sleep in the hay loft just to protect my weak willpower, but it's what I need to do.

ESME

Most mornings, Drazak takes his bow and arrow and leaves without another word to us. Han'zir is busier now than I've ever seen him, as if he's trying to make up for all the lazy days in the past. He tears out stalks that have been ravaged by soldiers, and shores up soil and fertilizer around those few that remain and are still able to produce this season. Occasionally I find him whispering to them, giving them little encouragements and telling them his secrets.

One afternoon, though, we've run out of things to do, and Drazak still hasn't returned, so I pick up my baskets and head out into the woods to scrounge up what I can. Han'zir stays behind to wait for Drazak to return, and the haunted look in his eyes is almost too much for me to bear.

Even he can't hide how defeated he is, how the pain of losing everything gnaws at him. He fakes smiles and forces himself to remain upbeat to keep us going, but underneath, he's hurting. I wish I could take it away, but all I can do is be there for him.

When I return from my trip, there's a fire going and Drazak is home. Again I try to take the smallest portion I can, but Han'zir insists I eat more. As the food falls into my belly, it fills me with guilt. Drazak is watching me over the fire, and his gaze is so intense, so piercing, that I have to look away. It makes my pulse race, my chest tighten and burn. What is he thinking? Does he feel the same deep pull towards me that I feel towards him?

I don't realize he's stood up until he's right in front of me. He kneels down and slides some of his food into my bowl with a grunt of annoyance. Before he can leave, though, I grab onto his dirty, torn pants.

"Thank you," I say quietly. I don't know if I'm thanking him for the food or for simply caring about me. He just nods gruffly, and pads back to his seat.

Maybe I should leave. I'm only a burden to them now, another mouth to feed with food that doesn't exist. And these strange feelings I have... they seem dangerous, like it would upset the balance here even more.

But can I really go? To my orc and my troll, I am a person, with thoughts and feelings—not an object to be used and abused like my master did, and someday thrown away.

Maybe if I can keep finding food, keep helping as much as I can, I won't feel so guilty whenever they feed me, whenever I have traitorous thoughts.

My head snaps up. Perhaps I can help in a small way. I get up quickly and jog back to the barn, with Han'zir calling my name after me. Up in the hay loft I dig around until I find the stash of food I've been keeping. Some has gone bad now, but not everything. I pull it down with me, tucked under my arm, and carry it back to the fire.

As I lay it all out in front of them, Han'zir's eyes are round, while Drazak's brows pull into a dark frown. There are nuts, fruit, dried meat, even some fried pork skin I saved, knowing I would need quick fats if I chose to leave.

"I'm sorry," I say, my hands trembling. "I'm sorry for taking it." I turn my head away, squeezing my eyes shut. I don't want to see their faces when they learn I've been stealing from them a little at a time.

But they jerk open when a hand lands on my shoulder. It's Han'zir, with a tender, sad look on his face.

"What is this, *keva*?" he asks me, his voice quiet.

"Food. I was... keeping it." Tears are welling up in my eyes. "I'm sorry." Drazak's face is even more tense as he looks over what I've brought.

"Were you going to leave?" His eyes find mine, and there's hurt in them. "Is that what this is?"

My mouth opens and closes while I search for the right answer.

"Oh, *keva*." Han'zir kneels down next to me. He wraps his arms around me, pulling me in tight against his chest. He's not angry at me?

But when I look up, Drazak looks furious. "Why?" he demands. "Why would you leave?"

"I..." My voice sticks in my throat. What can I possibly say? I gesture around at the devastated farm. "No food. Not enough."

Drazak's face falls. He surges off the log where he's been sitting and stalks towards us, and I cringe in preparation for him to hit me. Instead, I feel a calloused hand on my cheek.

"There is enough," Drazak says in a low voice, and his eyes are hot as flame when I look into them. "There will be enough."

His words wash over me like cool water. I cover his hand in mine and lean into his palm. He sighs, then pulls away to pick through what I've brought. He grabs an apple and arches an eyebrow, because we both know I took it from the bucket meant for the horses.

We're all quiet that night as we sit around the fire, looking into the flames for any sign of what our future holds.

HAN'ZIR

I'm not oblivious. How could I be, when I know Drazak better than I know myself? I'm not immune to Esme's significant charms, either. Now that I'm accustomed to her, to her presence, to her strange body and tiny face with the button nose, I find her... alluring. Exciting. Whenever I'm near her, whenever she smiles at me, my blood pumps a little faster, and I imagine it's the same for my orc, too.

He needs this, whatever strange thing is happening between them. I know it because I'm growing to need it myself. But we're different, him and I. I've always known this, but now it's as stark as a bird's shadow against the sky. He thinks with his body while I think with my heart. Even when he's grumpy with me, his cock recognizes me and shows me what's really inside him. He can never stay mad for long when deep down, he wants nothing more than me.

So I understand when I see it on his face, this bodily need for her. All of his strange behavior makes sense when I align it with her arrival, with each stage of our peculiar journey together.

One night, as Drazak's hands roam my body, skating over the plane of my abdomen and down to my groin, I stop him. I've known for a while now that not all of his mind is here with me when he's deep inside me, his teeth nipping at my neck. I know he's coping with what we've lost and the hard months we face ahead. I also know he's hungering, and the need grows more raw every day.

"What is it?" Drazak grumbles, reaching again for me. "Don't want me inside you tonight? You could fuck me, instead."

"It's not that." I turn around and place my hands on his shoulders sternly, then stare into his golden eyes, which are always red around the edges now. My poor orc, who holds everything inside until it chokes him. "Drazak... why do you really not want the puppy to sleep in the house?"

He blinks, then growls with irritation. "Why are we talking about this now?" His whole body becomes tense and hard. "What does it matter? We have bigger problems."

"I worry about her," I say. "Don't you?"

"Where would she sleep?" he asks, scoffing. "In our bed?"

I tilt my head. "Sure." Then I lean closer so we're tusk-to-tusk. "All kinds of fun things could happen if she slept in our bed."

I don't expect Drazak to hiss at me and pull away like I've burned him. "Don't be ridiculous." He narrows his eyes. "With the way you treat her, that would be like fucking a farm animal."

He turns over, and I'm too stunned by his ferocity to go after him. I don't say anything else, and he goes to sleep with his back turned towards me.

Drazak has always had a hard shell around him, but now I worry it will grow impassable.

I can't survive without him, and if he's going to get through this—like he must—the only thing that will give him enough hope to keep going is her.

CHAPTER 8

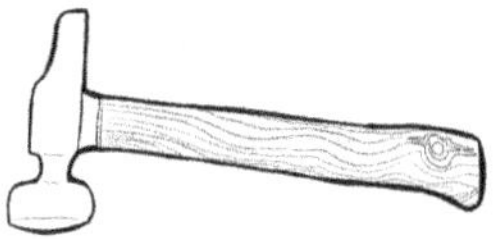

Of course I wanted nothing more than to agree. Yes, let her sleep in our bed with us, our little human. There we'll keep her warm when the cold weather comes, and I'll finally get to have her the way my body has been ravenously waiting for.

But Han'zir doesn't see her the way I do. He doesn't know the festering desire that's steadily growing until it threatens to consume me. He sees her as an object, a cute decoration. A pet.

The next morning, Esme is out early to do something, and not even Han'zir can tell me where she is. I hope she hasn't gone out again to hunt for berries. I brought home food so she would stop putting herself at risk that way. There's little else to do, and Han'zir is in an oddly off-kilter mood. I suppose I can't blame him, given everything, but I hadn't realized just how much I rely on his endlessly optimistic attitude to keep me afloat.

"Why don't you go and look for her?" he says, finally taking his eyes off the long stick he's been whittling to glance up at me. He can't shoot an arrow to save his life, but Han'zir's not bad with a spear.

"You could go with me." I survey his work. "I know you're just killing time."

He shrugs, then gets a glint in his eye. "No. I think you should go alone."

I raise an eyebrow, feeling like I'm being lured into a trap but I don't know what it is. Surely he doesn't know the truth. Then he waves me off and returns to his somber task.

So I wander the farm, thinking Esme must have found some other chore to keep her busy. She's always busy, always doing something to help. The longer I'm alone, the more I think about her body against mine when she embraced me, her soft breasts pressing into my belly, the sturdiness of her heart filling me with one need: to protect. My troll and my human, who are at greater risk now than they would be on any war front.

The barn is empty, and oddly, the fence the soldiers broke has been fixed. I wonder when she found time to do that? My path takes me through the pasture, which used to be dotted with cows but now lies empty, toward the river.

That's when I hear splashing. I duck behind the trees, walking closer only a few steps at a time in case it's some neighboring trollkin out for a swim. But then a laugh fills the air, like the jingle of gold coins. I would know it anywhere.

Still, I keep to the shadows as I approach the river. The two sets of clothes we once gave Esme are lying on rocks on the shore, drying out in the sun after being washed. So that's what she's been doing. Now she's playing in the water, chasing after what looks like minnows just under the surface. Of course she's naked as the day she was born, her cute little butt in the air as she dives again. She laughs when she misses, and I'm amazed she can have so much brightness in the face of so much endless darkness.

I'm drawn to her. There's nothing I can do to stop my feet as they carry me down from the tree cover to the bank of the river. She doesn't notice me at first, because while our human has a sweet heart, she isn't very observant. It's not until I start removing my shirt that she turns around and spots me.

"Drazak!" The excitement in her voice sends a thrill through me. She sinks down in the water, so her breasts are hidden under the surface, and a flush crosses her face. I'm not even in control of my hands as I fling the shirt to the side, then unbutton my trousers. Her big eyes grow wide, but she doesn't move.

I need to be in the water with her. Whether she runs or not, I need to feel her nearby, to drink her in even if it's just a small drop. She's the salve I need on all my burns and scars, on this hopelessness that's taken up a permanent home in my chest. My cock is already coming to life, having watched her chasing after fish, and imagining what that naked skin of hers might feel like against my own.

Esme's wide eyes travel down my body as I take another step into the river, and the flush deepens when she reaches my groin, where I'm growing thick and hard for her.

"Drazak...?" she asks, her gaze returning to my face. She looks confused, but her eyes are alive in a way they've never been before.

I don't think she hates what she sees.

Without answering I make my way deeper, and she stays where she is, floating underneath the gentle ripple of the water so all I can make out are the darker nipples at the tips of her round breasts. More than anything I want to touch them, to take one of those tiny nipples in my hand and then in my mouth. I want to know what she tastes like, because if it's anything like how she smells, I could sate my need by simply licking her soft skin.

My mind empties of everything that isn't Esme.

When I finally reach her the water is up to my waist, but her eyes still dart down to my cock where it lies under the surface. She doesn't back away, remaining steadfast, as if waiting to see what I have planned. I stoop down so I'm closer to eye-level with her. All of her light brown hair is wet and dark, clinging to her small head and long, shapely neck. I want to sink my teeth into her smooth throat. When I reach towards her, she doesn't move or even flinch. I tuck one of the wet strands behind her ear, then run my finger along the line of her cheekbone. She shivers, but I don't think it's from the cool water, not on a day like today.

I take in all of her face, how her chin is pointed, how her eyes are too big for her face and her nose is upturned at the tip. Her lower lip trembles as I lean closer, cupping her jaw in my big fingers. I don't realize how large I am until I'm near her, and then all I want to do is envelop her, wrap her up completely in myself and never let her go.

My hand travels of its own accord to her mouth, where I smooth over her lips with my thumb. Her eyes are even wider now, and I think the confusion has all left. She knows why I'm here, because she understands me. She knows me, somehow, even though we'd never met before she arrived.

Ever so slightly, her lips part, and her tongue darts out to lick the pad of my finger. My whole body heats up instantaneously. What if that tongue were elsewhere? What might she do with it? Then she brings my whole thumb into her mouth, and I know then exactly how it would feel, what it would look like, to put my cock between those plump lips.

I groan as she sucks on my thumb, her eyes never leaving mine. Has she been wanting me, too? That, to me, is a mystery. How could a small, gentle human want a big, ugly orc like me? But she brings me even deeper into her mouth, then draws out my thumb to suck on my forefinger, instead. My breath nearly stops in my throat as her wide eyes drift up to mine.

I need more. No, I have to have more.

I step closer, gently pulling away from her sweet, wet mouth to drop my hands under the water. There they find their way to her small breasts, which each fit more than neatly into my palms. Her eyes are still the size of saucers, disbelieving, even as she gasps with pleasure and her body bends into my touch. How do I make her believe?

I know one way. So I lean down and kiss her.

HAN'ZIR

She went down to the river to wash her clothes this morning, before Drazak dragged himself out of bed. He's never been a late sleeper, but this catastrophe has changed all of us.

So I decided to play a little game. I'm not quite certain what will happen when he's presented with this opportunity, and I want to find out.

I stay at a reasonable distance, keeping track of Drazak's shadow as he moves through the trees. I remain there, inside the tree cover, as he takes off his clothes. I'm surprised by such a bold move, but something about her seems to trigger a different part of him, a dominance I haven't seen before. The way he strides into the water, right towards her, makes me wonder if his pull to her is stronger than I thought.

I'm even more surprised when, his hands cupping her small breasts, he leans forward and kisses her. It's shocking to see him swoop down low and take her lips so confidently. I lean further forward, keeping myself hidden behind a wide tree trunk, as his hands explore her body. She's so different from either of us, with that soft swell of hip and the narrow ribcage, the small hands and curved thighs, and I'm entranced by the sight of him touching her. What would she feel like under *my* hands?

I wonder if he'll tell me.

His arms bring her in closer, wrapping all the way around her small body, and she lets out a gasp as Drazak's hand dips down between her thighs, seeking out what precious riches lie there.

Esme's head falls back and her mouth opens in a low moan, sending a tingle up my spine. My cock twitches at the sight of Drazak's big, naked body bent down over hers, and I wish I could be there with them. They're beautiful.

But perhaps this moment is theirs and theirs alone. Ducking my head to stay out of sight, I turn around and leave.

Esme

"Good *keva*," Drazak says as he drags his hand down my hip and then across my belly, testing out every inch of me, sampling it with his fingers. It fills me with pleasure to hear him say it, to know that I'm doing a good job, even though I'm not sure what exactly that job is. Though his cock is fully hard and pressed up against my other hip, so I guess I have a clue.

I never expected Drazak. When he appeared in the trees, I worried he might chastise me for some reason or another. Instead he simply watched me, and as he took off his clothes, I saw exactly what he wanted—and I knew I wanted it, too. Now that thick, sturdy body, the powerful belly and muscled chest is filling my head with every dirty thought it's possible to have. All this time I've been desperate for the big orc's approval, but perhaps what I really needed was this.

While his hands discover me, I do the same to him, raising my palm to his dark green skin. I test out the give only to find tough, dense muscle there. His gentle fingers dip downward, toward the cavity between my thighs, and one slides neatly between them. Oh, how just that tiny hint, that suggestion of what else he could do there, sets my body aflame. When I drag my hand past his nipple in response, Drazak bites his lip, and I'm drawn back up to his mouth. I've always liked the way his thick lips wrap around his tusks, drawing his lower jaw out, giving him a brutishness that strikes a chord in me, deep down inside.

This time I tilt my head up to bring our mouths together, and he crushes me against his body when he takes me. The way he kisses me is different from the way he kisses Han'zir—more forceful, like he's trying to consume me and bring me into himself.

Han'zir. My hands freeze, and I jerk away from that overwhelming kiss. I search Drazak's yellow eyes, trying to find the meaning behind this, why he's naked in the water with me with his cock eagerly nudging at my belly and hinting at where else it could be.

"*Keva?*" he says, brow furrowing at my withdrawal. He pulls me back in and, more eagerly this time, slips the pad of his finger between my folds. I can't hold in the quiet moan that escapes me.

"Wait." I'm breathing hard when I back away, and his hand falls to his side. "Han'zir." I shake my head, my stomach twisting. "You and Han'zir."

Drazak falls still. I'm embarrassed that I let it get this far before thinking of him. When I finally look up, I find Drazak's face hard and severe. He turns away from me, his shoulders now clenched tight around his neck and his hand balled up into fists. I back away further, now alarmed at what I've said, what it's set off inside him. I think of my master when he grew angry with me, when he got that look in his eye that told me it was time to run.

"Fuck," Drazak says, mouth set in a hard line. Then he shuts his eyes and breathes out, deeply. I stand there, waiting for what he's going to do next, readying myself to flee if I need to.

But he answers my question for me by heading straight for the shoreline, leaving me standing in the middle of the river. Cursing under his breath, he yanks his clothes back on, never once looking back at me. Then he rushes up the slope, towards the house.

I pick up my own clothes, still damp, and my hands tremble as I put them on. Then I trudge home, not believing what I've done.

Drazak is Han'zir's, not mine. I knew that, but still, I got carried away in him.

My guilt rises up until I'm drowned in its shadow, and then it crashes over me.

CHAPTER 9

HAN'ZIR

I'm surprised to see Drazak return not too much later. I expected they would be gone a while, but when I take in his dour expression, a thread of fear weaves through me. Did something happen?

Drazak runs a hand over his hair, glancing at me once with a furious look on his face before stalking past into the house, the door slamming behind him.

Esme returns a few minutes later, alone, and sits down on the log farthest away from me. She draws her knees together, crouching forward as if to make herself look smaller.

Something's gone wrong. This is definitely not what I intended.

I'm torn between which of them to comfort first. Drazak looked angry, so I'll leave him alone for now. He needs to cool off from whatever happened. Esme, on the other hand, doesn't know how to look for help when she needs it. She'll simply curl in on herself until someone rescues her.

I sidle up to her on the log, and reflexively, she flinches away. That's curious.

"Are you okay, puppy?" I ask, petting her hair. Her eyes squeeze shut, and now I'm certain that something awful has happened.

"I'm sorry." The words come out a whimper. "I'm sorry, Han'zir."

My hand pauses on her head. "Sorry?" I ask. Maybe they got into some kind of argument. "What for?"

Finally, she looks at me, and her eyes are red. She blinks away tears and says, "Drazak. I... We..." She's at a loss for words. After a moment she steels herself and says, "We touched. In the river. I'm sorry."

They touched? That's all? Finally, it occurs to me what probably happened. They got into the heat of the moment, and our little Esme felt guilty.

I should have expected that. Now I feel terrible for engineering something that would hurt her.

"Poor puppy." I scoot even closer and lean her head against my shoulder. "It's okay. You don't have to be sorry."

"But why?" She pulls away and looks at me accusingly, like I should be mad at her and she's angry that I'm not. "I'm bad. It was bad."

"You're not bad. Why would you say that?" I glance over at the house where I know Drazak is inside, surely loathing himself just as much as she is. "He's hot, right? Gorgeous." I tilt up her chin. "So kissable."

"Kissable?" she repeats.

I nod, then tilt her up even further, lowering my head until our noses are almost touching. I give her just the smallest peck on the lips, my skin grazing past hers and lighting me up like a match striking a flint.

"Kissable," I say.

While Esme sits there with her mouth slightly open, I get up and dust off my pants. "I'm not mad at you, puppy," I tell her. "You're good. All right?"

She looks utterly perplexed, but that's better than crying, so I leave her alone to go patch up the other broken fence.

DRAZAK

What have I done?

Han'zir is the best thing that's ever happened to me. Why would I even *risk* throwing it all away, just for a human?

Fuck. Esme isn't any human, and even I know that. She means so much more than that, to both of us, and that's what makes this even more fucking shameful.

When the door opens and Han'zir steps in, I want to sink into the earth.

"Hmm," he says, walking up behind me and dropping one hand on my shoulder. "The two of you seem upset."

"It's fine," I growl. I don't need him poking around, because then I'll have to tell him the truth, and who knows what he'll do then.

"Fine?" He slinks around the table and sits across from me. "Doesn't seem fine. Little puppy was nearly in tears. What did you do to her at the river?"

It takes a moment to click what he's said.

"How did you know she was down at the river?" I ask, my voice dropping low. He's the one who told me to go find her with that mischievous look in his eye. "Han'zir, what did you do?"

His careless shrug makes me want to strangle him. "I'm just trying to help," he says. "I know you want her. I just made sure you had the chance, that's all."

At this statement, all the dread seeps out of me, replaced by outrage. "You *set me up*?" I demand, getting to my feet. "You wanted me to be with her? To be with... someone else?"

He doesn't look anywhere near as upset as I am. "I wanted you to be happy, Drazak."

"I am happy!" I'm practically spitting now with my anger, which is probably not very convincing.

"I know you and she both need it." Han'zir shakes his head like I'm a fool. "Don't you?"

"No." I say it forcefully, almost desperately, because it's a lie. "I don't need anyone else but you."

He sighs, propping his elbow up on the table and leaning into it. There's a warm affection in his eyes. "That's one of the things I've always liked about you. You're loyal even when your cock has been hungering for just the opposite. For weeks now."

I'm taken aback. "How did you know?"

"How could I not know?" Han'zir stands up in front of me and sometimes I forget that he's taller, tall enough that I have to look up, and he's using all of that height now. "I understand, Drazak. You need her, or you wouldn't be getting hard every time she walks by you. You deserve one good thing."

Ugh, was I that obvious? No. I'm supposed to be angry right now, absolutely furious at his meddling.

"I understand, you know," he says, running a finger up one of my tusks, "how you feel about her. Because I feel it, too."

I blanch. "Feel what?"

He leans towards me, his lips almost brushing my ear. "That thirst, like you're parched and searching for water, and she's the lake."

How does he know exactly the way it felt to drink her and finally sate my need? I'm humiliated that he saw through me so easily.

And yet, much more makes sense now. I've always thought he lavished affection on her the way someone would a dog or a cat, but now I see it—the way he finds excuses to touch her, how he always thinks of her needs when I don't, how he laughs and plays with her.

"Fuck," I hiss. "Really? This whole time, and you didn't tell me?"

He shrugs. "You didn't tell me, either. Besides, the way you need her is... different." His eyebrow arches suggestively.

So he knows just how desperate I am to fuck her, how my body longs for nothing else than to wrap around her and bury myself in her, and then do it again, and again, filling her up with my seed until—

I groan and pull away from him, rubbing a hand down my face. "She's *human*, Han'zir!"

He shrugs. "That doesn't change anything, does it?"

"Of course it does!" How can he be so daft? "It can't work with her. This is not a permanent thing. You knew it, I knew it. Someday someone is going to find her here."

"We'll make sure they don't." Unexpectedly, his face hardens. "I'm not going to give her up. Are you?"

I gape at him. "It's not a choice!"

"Yes, it is. We can really give her a home here, with us, or we can send her on her way. Those are the choices."

When he says it, my throat tightens up and my skin turns hot. "Send her on her way?" I ask, wincing when my voice cracks.

"Let her go. Tell her to shoo. Send her back to the rest of her kind, where she'll be safe. The frontier is close enough that we could get her there." He looks at me with a surprising sternness in his face. "Nothing else is fair. We either ask her to stay, with us, if that's what she wants... or we ask her to go."

The idea of her leaving the farm fills me with an ugly, aching dread. No, I need her here, with me. With us. Where she belongs.

Esme

I really have no idea what to make of it all.

Han'zir wasn't angry at me, like I had quite reasonably expected him to be. Instead, he reassured me, and then left to speak with Drazak. I wonder what the orc has told him about what we did down at the river.

A fresh wave of humiliation passes through me. The worst part of all of it? How much I liked it. How much I wanted him.

Then there's the way my body reacted when Han'zir kissed me, ever so faintly. The ghost of a kiss and the promise of a future one. It set fire to a different part of me, but these flames were soft and warm and wrapped around my heart.

I drop my head into my hands, wishing I knew what's come over me, what's wrong with me that I want not one, but *two* trollkin. They're supposed to be my sworn enemies, or so our major said. They are the very creatures I'd been sent into war to kill, and yet in the river, kissing Drazak with my body flush against his, that thick cock speaking its desires to me, we weren't enemies at all. Being close to him felt like having every last one of my cravings fulfilled, like eating one of the beautiful cakes I used to always make for the master's wife.

And being with Han'zir? It's as easy as breathing. He has an uncanny ability to anticipate what I'm going to do, what object I need handed to me, even how I'm feeling. It's like there's a channel between us that he's fully tapped into, and I haven't even breached the outer layer yet.

What a miserable person I am, to be thinking of both of them this way. They were fine and happy before I came, but I'm like a tornado that blew through and devastated everything in its path.

Maybe I should go now, before I can be punished.

"*Keva?*" I glance up to find Han'zir standing over me, Drazak with his arms crossed behind him. They must be here to confront me. "Come with us."

I take in Han'zir's calm, encouraging face, then turn to Drazak, whose mouth is stiff and set. My shoulders curl as I imagine what they're going to say. Will they ask me to leave?

With a sigh, Drazak stalks over to me, slips his arms under me, and sweeps me up like I weigh nothing. I squeal, but he doesn't put me down.

"Shh." He pauses, then leans down and brushes his lips over mine. The gesture is so intimate and yet so casual, I'm stunned by it. And right in front of Han'zir.

Behind us, the troll chuckles.

When he carries me into the house, Drazak doesn't put me down by the fire pit like I expect. He carries me into their bedroom, where he crouches down and sets me on the pile of blankets and furs they sleep on. He sits next to me, and Han'zir joins him.

Now I'm even more perplexed with the two of them together, Han'zir leaning on Drazak's shoulder affectionately. It doesn't seem like anyone is angry. In fact, the troll's eyes look simply alight, but he's holding himself back.

"*Keva*," Drazak begins. "Do you want to stay in the house with us?"

What? I blink at him, and then turn to Han'zir to see if I'm missing something. He nods eagerly.

"...Yes?" I say uneasily, not sure if they're being serious.

Han'zir grins. "Good."

That's all? I'm sleeping in the house now and not the barn? But I sense there's more.

Han'zir moves to the other side of the bed so now I'm flanked by them, and there he lies down next to me. If I weren't so nervous right now, it would feel wonderful to have him so close. "And what do you think, *keva*, of us?"

I stare at him, trying to sort through his question. "Of you?" It only takes one look at Drazak for hot blood to rush into my face, because immediately I think of him naked, walking into the river in all his glory, that cock between his legs swollen for me. I have to stare down at my hands because it makes my hips tight and my blood tingle.

"Ah," says Han'zir knowingly. "So you like him. And what about me?" He sits up so he's leaning over me, and runs a hand down my cheek.

"You...?" I wish I knew more words, damn it. "You... you're good. You're very good." I lean into his palm, hoping that he can hear and see and understand how I feel about him. How he makes me happy, how he lights up every room he enters, how his companionship means everything to me.

Han'zir chuckles. "Very good?" His head drifts down closer, until his mouth is almost on top of mine. How I want him to close that gap between us. How I would love to get to really feel him, fully, and not just a promise.

"And kissable," I say.

Han'zir grins.

"Kiss her," Drazak barks. The command takes me by surprise, but that's quickly swallowed up as Han'zir does what he's told and lowers his lips to mine. They settle sweetly there, applying a soft pressure that raises every hair on my skin. My body reacts of its own accord, my chest rising up to meet his as he brings my lower lip into his mouth, sampling it, tasting it. His arm loops underneath me, pulling me even closer until my breasts are squashed against him.

Oh, to be kissed by Han'zir. Everything about him is a soft caress, and it sparks a tiny flame inside me when his lips gently pry mine apart, seeking a way in. I can trust him, more than anyone in this world, so I don't hesitate to allow him through.

He groans against me as his tongue investigates my mouth, exploring every part of me. I'm lost in it, forgetting where we are, when we are, how we are. I've been kissed before, mostly by Benny, the other help, and then it was sloppy and feverish. There's no comparison. It's only once I hear Drazak grunt that I pull away, suddenly overwhelmed by embarrassment. We did that right in front of him.

But the orc's yellow eyes are heated, his pupils dilated to fill his whole iris. His hand smooths across his groin, where a noticeable bulge lies underneath his pants. He nods at me.

"Keep going."

Han'zir shifts his body so we're lying side-by-side, facing one another, then he retakes my mouth. I gasp against him as he invades deeper this time, his arm keeping me flush against him. His tusks brush my cheeks as he brings me further into himself, and his hands wander down my sides, smoothing over my dress. His teal-blue skin is soft under my palms, and I touch him in return, exploring his sinewy arms, tracing the shape of his wide chest and narrow hips. He shudders under me, and then something firm and pulsing rubs my thigh.

He's turned on by me? I pull away from our kiss, my breathing heavy and my body alive with sensation. I thought certainly Han'zir only had eyes for Drazak, but there's a deep, aching lust written on his face.

He wants more. Of *me*.

CHAPTER 10

HAN'ZIR

I want her. I need her. I've felt affection for her, of course, and being near her makes my blood sing. But none of that compares to right now, to feeling Esme's body, tasting her on my lips, hearing her gasps.

Our puppy is so yielding under my hands and yet so full of passion, returning my kisses just as eagerly, her hands reveling in my shape. If I gave in, if I let this sprouting desire take over, I would surely lift up her dress and bury myself inside her.

But that's not how I want this first time to go. Now that I've shown her that I'm not angry at her, that I'm not jealous, I need to have patience for the rest. Besides, it will be Drazak who enjoys her that way first. They need each other, and I will be content to watch until their fire has turned all this kindling to ash. I will have my place when they're sated.

When I draw back from our kiss, Esme's eyes flutter open, and I'm delighted by the rosy color in her cheeks. Her lips look well-loved and her chest is heaving, meaning I've done my job of preparing her.

My gaze connects with Drazak's, and he responds to my mischievous smile with a nod. He understands.

When he lies down on the bed on her other side, Esme flashes me a look of surprise. She tries to turn over to face him, but his arms have already wrapped around her from behind, his calloused hands caressing her breasts over her dress. Her eyes dart up to mine, as if expecting a reprimand. So I kiss her lips again, sweetly, and then her forehead. I nuzzle her hair while Drazak's fingers drift farther down, smoothing over her belly and then her rounded hips. When he reaches the hem of her dress, he slips underneath. Esme jumps in surprise, so I kiss her again, holding her cheeks in my hands. Drazak joins me in lavishing attention on the back of her neck, her collar, her shoulder. He crushes her hips against his, and she lets out an "Oh!" of pleasure.

I watch as he slides her dress up, his big hand nearly eclipsing her thigh, and I get even harder—which I didn't realize was possible at this stage. Now the hem is up on her hips, revealing that wide pelvis and the patch of hair that lies at the juncture of her legs. I told myself I'd leave them to it and watch from the sidelines, but my curiosity is too powerful. I've seen trollesses and orcesses naked before, but never felt particularly inclined to explore them myself. I want to know what lies there, what my Drazak craves so much.

"Open for me, puppy," I whisper to her, my hand slipping down to those exposed thighs. Without hesitation she obeys, her legs just barely parting for me, but it's enough for one of my thick fingers to slide between them.

My entire body shudders at what I find there. She is soft, so soft. The curly hair continues on, thinner and finer, protecting that delicate sex underneath. All I feel at first are two folds of skin, leading down to something even more fascinating: a small dip, where my finger abruptly meets moisture. My cock surges against my pants at this tiny taste, this foreign but exciting discovery. I draw back, exploring the folds again, delving between them with just the pad of my finger. Esme's hips jerk under me, and she lets out a breathy moan when I find a little nub hidden inside. It's like searching for buried treasure, where the reward is her bliss.

"You're so warm," I say, returning again to that moist place farther down. I duck gently inside it, and again Esme's body responds, her hips shifting to allow me in. "So warm and wet." I retake her mouth while Drazak squeezes her small, round ass, then pulls her dress up even further to give him access to her breasts.

"Because she wants us," he answers, and sucks in a breath as he takes her nipples in his fingers. "Don't you, puppy?"

She nods rapidly as she grinds against my finger, urging it deeper. "I want you," she whimpers, and the sound sends a jolt of lightning straight to my cock. Fuck. Suddenly I wonder if I'm going to be able to let Drazak take her first at this rate, because this blistering hot, soaked place between her legs is screaming my name.

No. Their bond needs healing after today, and I know just where I will fit.

To spare myself the temptation, I pull away from our Esme, and she lets out a sound of protest. I shake my head and kiss her cheeks.

"Drazak," I tell her. "Go to him."

Her eyes search me for some hidden meaning, so I rub the tip of my nose against hers. "It's all right, puppy. I want to watch you."

Her breath halts and her mouth opens at this suggestion. "Watch me?" she repeats. I grin at her and gesture for her to go. "Oh."

With one last uncertain look, she turns over on the bed to face my orc, and the desire and relief on his face is enough for me. While he pulls her into him, I slide off my pants, taking my cock in hand, ready for a moment I never realized I was waiting for.

Esme

I still don't quite believe that Han'zir *wants* me to be with Drazak, that the idea turns him on, that he wants to... watch us.

Embarrassment burns my cheeks as I face Drazak, the orc who approached me in the river, who held me to his chest and kissed me like he was starving and I was his food. The orc who's watched over us, sacrificed for us, protected us. He sits up long enough to peel off his shirt, and then his pants follow along, ending up in a pile on the floor. He doesn't say a word as he yanks my dress up the rest of the way, nearly tearing it off of me as he pulls it over my head. Then I'm bared to him, and to Han'zir, too. I've only been with one man, Benny, but it was in the dark of night—a tryst purely of one body's need for another. I took very little pleasure in it. I certainly didn't see him, and neither did he see me.

Now I am very, very seen.

Over my shoulder, Han'zir sits up, taking his big cock in one hand. It's even bigger than Drazak's, as thick as my forearm, and a powerful shudder travels from my throat to the base of my spine.

When Drazak kisses me, it's a very different kind of kiss than Han'zir's. No, it's fierce and ravenous, his teeth nipping my lips, his tongue filling my mouth and seizing mine. I can sense his urgency in every squeeze of his hands on my flesh, the way he grips my butt and fondles my nipples. Suddenly I, too, feel impatient and starved, overcome by the need that's been building in me ever since he pressed his cock against me in the water—perhaps since long before that. I've never ached for someone like I do for him. I know where Drazak fits, where he belongs, and that's inside me.

I don't want to wait, not after Han'zir paid such close attention to me, but Drazak doesn't seem to care. He spreads my thighs with one demanding hand and finds my clit right away. His touch gentles as he plays with it, brushing it from side to side, and I moan and buck. After he's tormented me for what feels like eons, he drags that hand lower, and presses one finger inside me.

"Drazak," I whimper. I didn't expect how big it would be, but together, their touches and kisses have loosened me, and it slides inside. A cry bursts out of me, and Drazak bears down on my mouth with another powerful kiss. His finger starts to pump in and out, whisked along by how I'm growing ever wetter, and he devours my gasps.

"Yes, *keva*," he grunts, playing with my breasts and tugging on my nipples hard. Each point of contact pours more oil on the fire of my need until my whole body is rocking in tandem with his hand, making Drazak tense up against me, his cock nudging ever more insistently against my thigh. Then he retreats, returning to my sensitive clit, which he rubs even harder than before. Behind me, I hear Han'zir groan, and when I glance over he's stroking his cock so hard he's nearly strangling it.

"I wanted to go slow," Drazak growls in my ear, "but I can't."

I nod, because I understand. I want to be joined with him the way my body has been craving. It's a need I've never felt before, a consuming urge that now threatens to boil over.

Suddenly Drazak grabs me by both arms and turns me over so I'm lying flat on my back. He swings his leg across until he's on top of me, the weight of his hips over mine keeping me rooted to the earth. He shoves his cock between my thighs, groaning as they ruthlessly squeeze him. Pausing to take a few deep breaths, Drazak looks down at me, his body even bigger now than I remember it being. For a moment his usual stern look fades, and a smile pulls his tusks up on his cheeks. His hard brow, his barrel belly, the set of his jaw—I whimper, wanting him, desiring nothing else but him. Beside us, Han'zir groans.

"Fuck her, Drazak," he demands, and all of his usual playfulness has been replaced by pure longing. "I need to see you inside her. Esme, you want him, don't you?"

There is, perhaps, nothing else in the world more erotic than my troll insisting that my orc shove his cock into me. I think it is far beyond my wildest dream, and surely this isn't real.

"Yes," I say breathlessly. "Please." Drazak's yellow eyes lock onto mine with a feral intensity, then he nods and pulls my thighs wide, gripping me so tight I wonder if I'll bruise. His fingers travel down, and now instead of just one there are two squeezing inside me, demanding that I open wide for him. My head falls back and my pussy is both fighting him and crying for him. He gathers up all of my wetness, slathering his fingers in it, and once more works them inside me.

Now my moan is a cry, and Drazak falls down onto one elbow, gasping with effort. "I need you, *keva*," he mutters in my ear, drawing his tongue across the shell of it as he strokes inside me, finding a delicious, sensitive spot that makes my very being ache with pleasure. And then suddenly, there is a third finger, and this time it's followed by a pinch of discomfort. I wince, and Drazak stops.

"Wait one moment," says Han'zir. He presses his body to my side, running his hands over my breasts, gently cupping each one in his hand. His lips traverse my cheek, then my jaw and my throat. His cock nudges at my thigh, sending a shock of thrill through me. "Let him in, sweet *keva*."

It's as if my body is a puppet on his strings, because Drazak's three fingers are now fully encased in me, twisting and spreading to open me for him. While Han'zir devotes himself to touching me, my orc removes his hand, and draws my thighs apart even further. Then he kneels between them, his dark green cock lying across my mound. His eyes find mine as he drags it downward, over my sensitive button and back again, that soft head escaping the skin protecting it to rub over me in a harsh, feverish motion. His gaze is piercing, intent only on me.

"Please," I say again. My words make him moan, and he shoves his cock down even further. Without warning, the soft tip dips inside me.

Now I understand his three fingers. It's too much, too big, too everything, even though I want it—crave it—more than food or water or shelter. I wriggle my hips, trying to bring him inside me, but Drazak holds me still, just waiting at the edge. Han'zir leans in close and reaches down between us, his hand finding my stretched edges and stroking up and down them.

"Take him, *keva*," Han'zir whispers to me, splaying his fingers to spread my pussy wide.

"Yes, yes," I answer. Drazak lets out an animalistic grunt as he pushes in.

I can't stop the cry that comes out of me when that fat, swollen head breaks through. In the same breath that it pinches, it also feels like perfect bliss. Drazak silences me with his lips, plunging his tongue inside me the way his cock is filling me as he sinks in deeper. He groans, pausing his entry, and withdraws himself again.

"Drazak!" It comes out a whine, and my orc chuckles to himself as once more he retreats, and then pushes in only part way, taunting me, teasing me, and soon I'm writhing underneath him, begging for more. Han'zir's mouth is open as he watches, his cock leaking from the tip, and it only makes me more desperate to have Drazak inside me.

"Do you want it?" he asks, rocking his hips in and out, barely breaching me. "Do you want all of me?"

"Yes, please. Please." I need nothing else in this whole cruel world besides him.

My orc leans down, kissing the planes of my face, whispering

Trollkin words I can't understand. And then in one smooth motion, he thrusts in.

My cry fills up the room, and Han'zir gasps. Drazak pitches down, his face in my neck as he yanks himself out, and then fills me again, deeper and harder this time. Somewhere inside me there's a place carved out just for him, and when he settles there, buried as far as my body will allow, it feels as if a broken pot is putting itself back together, the shards clicking into place.

Beside us, Han'zir suddenly gets off the bed, but I'm so lost in the feeling of Drazak that I don't notice where he's going. Slowly my orc starts to move again, never leaving me, simply reeling his hips back an inch or two and then thrusting into my depths, stretching me so wide I don't know how I don't burst apart. Every single stroke triggers a shock of agonizing pleasure, so intense that my body gives as much as it squeezes, softening as much as it clamps down tight around him. Drazak slides a hand under my hips, lifting me up, allowing him even deeper, and he groans as he bites into the flesh of my shoulder.

"Drazak," I moan, wrapping both my arms tight around his neck because I need to hold onto him, otherwise I might float away.

"*Keva*," he grunts back, pressing his face against me, his curved tusks biting into my skin. As our bodies meld closer and closer together, I find I'm missing something, that a piece of our structure is absent.

That's when I see Han'zir over Drazak's back, his face taut with bare, animalistic hunger. He kisses his shoulder as Drazak sinks inside me again, rubbing the orc's body with his even larger hands.

"There you are," I whisper, reaching towards him. When my five fingers meet Han'zir's four, they wrap around each other, and suddenly each of Drazak's strokes feels even more immense, more wonderful. When he looks down at me, his eyes are wide.

It's as if the whole world is shifting around us, rearranging to make room for us, and we are fitting together in the place we were always meant to be.

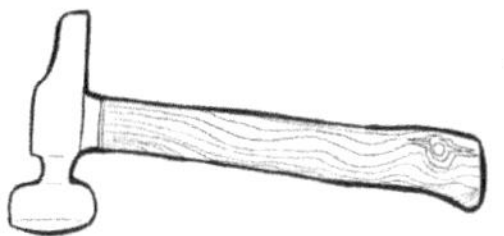

CHAPTER 11

DRAZAK

How it feels to be inside our girl. To fill her, to be squeezed and clenched by her, to look upon her small face and to smother her in my affection—it is unparalleled.

Or I thought that it was, until Han'zir steps behind me, his hands traversing my back and my hips as I thrust into her, taking her, claiming her as ours. My troll's hands wander downward, over my ass to where I'm buried inside Esme's sopping wet cunt. There he takes my balls in his hand, massaging them just the way I like.

"Fuck," I groan. "I'm going to explode if you do that."

"That's not all I'll do," Han'zir growls back, and there's a headiness in his voice, a low rumble I've never heard before. Watching us has stirred something up in him, too, and it is large and fearsome. While I drown in Esme's sweet, wet, perfect cunt, Han'zir snatches the oil off the table beside our bed, coating his fingers in it, and runs them down my backside.

I know what he plans to do. I groan as my cock is swallowed up, as Esme moans and cries underneath me, as Han'zir finds the puckered hole between my cheeks. He slides a finger inside me, and his hand is trembling with his overflowing need. It takes everything in my power not to go off immediately. But I have work still to do on our Esme, even as her cries climb and her small channel tightens. I slow my feverish pumping so that Han'zir can widen my ass further, teasing me open for him. I long for that discomfort that will come when his cock fulfills its purpose, because it might be my only salvation.

"Drazak," my troll murmurs into my shoulder as he slathers himself up with even more oil, and rubs his cock all around my entrance. "Watching you two, you are beautiful." His hand grazes over both of us, caressing us, as his cock nudges its way inside me. "All I've ever wanted."

Han'zir has never spoken to me with such reverence. Something inside him is changing. Our beautiful Esme opens her eyes, staring up at me in confusion as to why I've slowed our pace. Then she sees Han'zir behind me, and her mouth falls open.

When my troll thrusts into me, only shallowly, my whole body bucks. I ram myself deep in Esme's cunt, moaning at the overwhelming sensation of my cock inside her and Han'zir inside me. I bite down hard on my lip so I don't burst, and slow my thrusts as my troll slowly works his way in, searching out the place where he belongs, just as I am now. He grunts and falls forward against my back, his chest already heaving. He buries his face in my neck as I start to move once more inside our Esme, my cock so slick with her that it glides in and out. Han'zir groans again as he settles where he belongs, his hands digging into my hips as he starts to pump. Now he guides our movements, each motion of his body triggering one in mine, as if we are both fucking Esme together.

I will make sure she never wants to leave us. I will fill her up with my seed and so will Han'zir fill her up with his, and I will make sure not a drop of it leaks out. Maybe she is small and human, but we will try our hardest to seed her, and should we get lucky... Oh, imagining her round with Han'zir's whelp, her breasts dripping as we fuck her, my mind and my cock and my soul are all ablaze.

I close my eyes and lose myself in the feel of both of them, my perfect two. Now I can sense each of them near me. Where once Han'zir felt out of my reach, together with Esme at this moment, I can touch him at last. As she slides into the place where she fits, so does Han'zir, and the three pieces all snap together as they form the picture that is us.

My mates.

Two of them. That is why Han'zir never felt the mate bond with me before—we were always waiting for her, our Esme. She was meant for us as much as we were meant for her. And now we are complete. I know that this was always meant to happen, that every painful thing that's led us here was for a reason.

When the realization strikes me, I can't hold back any longer. I look down into her huge brown eyes, and they are just as wide and surprised as mine. Then they close and her whole body tightens, clamping down on my cock so hard that it's only Han'zir stroking inside me that keeps me going. I roar as my peak takes me, as I fill up thick and swollen inside her, as I shoot out everything I have to give and more. She cries out our names, her head falling back as Han'zir fucks me harder and harder. He moans raggedly, shoving himself deep one more time, striking that place inside me that only he can reach, and I bellow as I pump even more seed inside Esme's dripping cunt. She rocks and moans, her body seizing as another furious climax sweeps her under. Han'zir echoes her cries as he jettisons all of himself inside me, and collapses against my back.

Now, they are mine. My everything.

HAN'ZIR

I'm not sure if I imagined what just happened. When I pull myself free of Drazak's beautiful ass, my cock slick with my seed, he turns to me and right then, I know we felt the same thing.

Esme. She is ours and we are hers, and each other's. The mate bond I've always longed for was right here. We were simply waiting for her to arrive. I kiss him, hard, harder than I ever have, and drop a hand to his rapidly-beating heart. He holds it there for a moment, panting against me. Then I stumble to the bed and collapse onto it alongside them. Drazak's thick seed is seeping out of her, so I gather it with my fingers and press it back in, and she moans under me.

"Can't let any of Drazak's gift escape," I whisper to her. Drazak nods in agreement. Already his cock is stiffening again. He is an animal, my orc. Perhaps I should let him fuck me next.

But he is exhausted, too, and Esme gasps for air a few times as he rolls off of her. I drag my hand over her chest to Drazak's and back again. He turns onto his side to curl around Esme, linking his arm with mine across her belly. Today I think I've seen him at both his most primal and his most tender. I am fascinated to find out what else I will learn about him, this orc who I thought I fully understood.

Now that we are mates, the true gate will open for me.

I'd always thought it strange and cruel that fate, or whatever higher power chooses these things, wouldn't let me find it in Drazak. But now I understand.

"Han'zir?" Esme whispers, her body fully relaxed, her eyes barely open. "Drazak?"

"Hmm?" Drazak murmurs.

"Yes, puppy?" I ask.

"Thank you." She covers our arms with her tiny hands and squeezes them. "I am home."

Drazak and I exchange a look over her head. I had wondered if a human could be imprinted, too, or if only the two of us were bound by mating. Now I think we have our answer.

"You are," Drazak answers, tucking her head under his chin.

"You will always be with us," I tell her, running my palm over her body. She nods and smiles, her eyes falling closed, her breathing turning slow and steady.

"Drazak?" I whisper to him.

I didn't realize he was falling asleep until he twitches at the sound of his name. "What?"

"Do you think we can put a whelp in her?" I breathe Esme in deeply, not yet ready to sleep and forget all the shining, perfect edges of this moment. Tomorrow will be the next day, and not all the details will be as firm in my mind as they are right now.

His eyebrows raise. "I don't know. She's human. But the thought did cross my mind." Then a troubled look comes over him. "What if we could?"

"Well, then, I'd want to. One of us." I cover Drazak's hand with mine.

But that concerned look on his face doesn't leave. "We can't." He glances down at her, and his expression softens into something else, something I can't identify. "Outside this bed, Han, everything is fucked. We are ruined. I don't know if we'll ever recover."

"Of course we will." I don't share his pessimism. To me, what happened here is a sign that we're on the right path. "We'll make it through the winter. Don't worry."

"How can I not worry?" He grits his teeth together, trying to stay quiet so he doesn't wake her. "Especially when you're talking bullshit about whelps? Not to mention—"

I lovingly put my hand over his mouth, silencing him.

"That's for tomorrow." Esme lets out a tiny sound, disturbed in her sleep by Drazak's tone. "If we can find our way through this to the answer, then we can surely find our way through anything."

In his eyes I can make out a glimmer of my hope reflected back at me, and I thank little Esme for coming into our lives, because I don't know what would have been left of him otherwise.

CHAPTER 12

My trollkin speak quietly as I hover on the edge of dreams, not quite fading into them. Drazak is worried about something, but I'm too far into sleep to comfort him. I hope that he isn't worried about me, because nothing will ever trouble me again.

Drazak is up before either of us the next morning, which bodes well. Perhaps, despite everything, things might return to normal—or as normal as they can be.

Thanks to the hog he hunted, we'll have enough sustenance for a while, but meat isn't enough to tide us over. I want to go farther afield to look for berries and nuts and greens.

"Come with me?" I ask Han'zir, carrying the baskets I usually take foraging. I know my orc and my troll don't like me going alone like this, so perhaps if I'm accompanied, Drazak won't frown on it.

Han'zir cocks his head, then looks around for Drazak, who's fixing up a piece of farm equipment he thinks he can sell. His brow is furrowed in concentration, his hands covered in grease as he fits a nut and wrenches it on.

"All right," Han'zir says, hopping off his tree perch. "Let's go." He whispers something in Drazak's ear as he slips by, and our orc mutters something in return before going back to his work.

As we head off into the trees, Han'zir takes my hand between his big fingers, and I love the way his hair shines pure blue in the sunlight. We reach the edge of the meadow and head off into the woods, walking along the river.

"There are other farms out here," he says. "But I know where they are. Still, we should be careful." I understand enough words now that I can make sense of most of it. I'm glad he's with me today.

It's hot out, and soon even under the tree cover we're both sweating. I brought one water skin, but we're forced to stop after a few hours and refill it. Only half of one basket is filled because much of what's out here has already been picked over. When we reach the river, Han'zir starts taking off his clothes without saying a word to me. Before I can blink, he leaps into the cold water stark naked.

"Come in, *keva*," he calls to me, flicking some in my direction.

"We are hunting," I tell him.

"And we need a break! It's too hot. So come on."

Pleased at the idea of spending some quality time with my troll, I take off my dress and join him in the water. He kisses me between bouts of splashing, and soon his cock is hard and stiff, and his face shifts from fun and playful to predatory. He picks me up and carries me out of the river, then gathers up all our clothes into a makeshift bed.

"Can I have you for myself this time?" he asks me, laying me back on it as if I'm a delicate doll.

I giggle. "Yes." I'll gladly hoard Han'zir for a while.

But instead of putting his cock in me, as I expect him to, he pulls my legs apart and peers down between them.

"What are you doing?" I ask when he doesn't move to touch me. No, he's simply staring at my most private place with wide eyes.

"Learning," he says. With a tentative gentleness, he runs his finger along my folds. I decide to let him do it, but it's hard to push down the humiliation I feel at being so exposed. Still, there's only keen interest in his eyes as he brushes over my clit, causing me to spasm. He does it again, and then again, until he's feverishly rubbing me and I'm writhing under his hands. When he gets too forceful, I stop him, panting.

"*Keva*," he says, "you smell too good." He leans in even closer and breathes me in, simply savoring it. And then most unexpectedly, his tongue brushes over me.

I gasp with surprise and pleasure, and he repeats the motion, going much more softly with his mouth. He explores me with his hand while he licks me, investigating the slit underneath. He slides one finger into me, and after bringing all of Drazak's cock inside me last night, he fits right in.

Oh, there's nothing like the feeling of my troll between my legs, lavishing me with his lips, tantalizing me with his hand, driving me steadily upward and upward.

"Your cunt is delicious," he says with wonder, pausing in his attack. Then he gets a wicked smile on his face, and buries his mouth in my pussy, sucking and licking and tormenting it in all manner of delightful ways. The pleasure is so intense that tears bite at the back of my eyes, and I'm writhing and moaning underneath him. When I finally crest the hill and even my neck is taut with unspent pleasure, something inside me bursts, and a gush of liquid rushes out of me. I gasp and pull away, concerned—but Han'zir doesn't let me. No, he keeps me in place with his hands, drinking up everything I have to give. When he's finished he's panting, and as he sits up, I find his cock thick and heavy and swollen a dark blue.

"I want to be inside you, *keva*," he says, licking his lips. His face is wet with me. "Please."

Of course I want that more than anything else right now. Instead of answering, I reach out for his cock and stroke it, drawing a low groan from his lips. Then I tilt my hips up toward him and drag the head of him through the slickness between my legs. His breaths are coming faster as he takes it by the root and guides his cockhead down. There's a fiery anticipation in his eyes as he watches it slide inside me.

He's even bigger than Drazak, and it's only thanks to his very eager attentions that even his head can fit. I moan wildly as it demands I open for him. "Oh, you are beautiful," he tells me, pausing to rub my clit. I cry out sharply, and encouraged, he presses in further. His eyes roll back in his head and he stops, taking halting breaths. "And you feel so good, I might just go off early."

There's even more of him to take, so much that not all of his cock can fit inside me. Han'zir is mesmerized by us, by the place where he's stroking in and out of me. He runs his fingers over my stretched lower lips, testing different angles on my clit. But as his motions speed up and a flame catches in my belly, he loses himself in the pleasure. Soon he's slamming into me, my thighs hiked up over his hips, his hands caressing my breasts and pulling my nipples. He drops down to lick them while he takes me, and I bury my hands in his hair, trying not to come apart.

"Do you know what happens when I fill you up?" he asks me, slowing down his strokes but delving even deeper, pulling himself almost to the edge of me before plunging back in. "When I get all my seed inside you?" The blistering glory of his cock makes it hard for me to find words.

"What happens?" I ask between gasps, and already that low, pulsing sensation is growing, spreading, firing off volleys of bliss across my body.

"Well..." He groans, dropping forward so his mouth is only inches away from mine. "Maybe, if we're lucky..." I tighten around him, and another fearsome cliffside rushes towards me. "If we're lucky, I'll put a whelp in you. A sweet, happy one. One we can take care of together, all three of us."

Whelp? I don't have time to think about this word because a volcanic heat takes me over, surging through me. I twine my legs around him, trying to pull him in close as I can, because my soul is screaming out for his. My cries echo in the trees.

"You feel so good, *keva*," he moans, plunging into me again and again, whipping up that heat into a bonfire until I'm sobbing out his name and drawn tight around him. "You are perfect. You are my heart."

Some of these words I know and some I don't, but I feel the meaning of them deep in my bones, in the place where the three of us are all bound together.

When I finally burst, my vision blurs, and Han'zir lets out a helpless groan into my ear. He thrusts hard, once more, twice more, before emptying himself inside me. His hips jerk with the sheer power of his finish, and he drops down onto his elbows, his breath mingling with mine.

"Thank you," he says, rubbing our noses together. "Thank you, *keva*."

It's late by the time we get back with our findings, which were rather slim, especially given how much we ate along the way. But it's enough to supplement the boar, and tomorrow I'll try again in another direction.

I enjoy the change in Drazak's face when I bring back the walnuts he likes, and he brushes a hand down my spine to the swell of my butt. "Thank you," he says, and the praise fills me up with pleasure and satisfaction.

Despite our small dinner, Han'zir is all smiles, and Drazak arches his eyebrow at me in question. I can't help my cheeks getting hot just thinking about what we did at the riverbank.

"Did you fuck our little *keva*?" Drazak asks him with a smirk.

Han'zir shrugs coquettishly. "Maybe. She just looked so pretty, it was impossible not to. Besides, we have to work hard if we're going to get a whelp in there."

Drazak's smile falls a little, and now I really want to know what this word means.

"Whelp?" I ask.

The two of them exchange a look.

"You know, how a chicken lays an egg?" Han'zir says.

"You want me to lay eggs?" I ask, a little horrified.

Both of them laugh at this, and it's wonderful to see Drazak laugh. I could make him laugh all day long.

"No, not quite." Still snorting, Han'zir wipes his face. "But, you know. A little troll or a little orc. Whichever of us gets lucky." He winks at Drazak, whose green face turns even darker green.

That's what it means. A baby. That's what they're after?

I laugh. I can't help it. The idea is just too ridiculous, but after I've gotten over my chuckle at their expense, I find they're both looking at me with frowns. "What?" I say. "Humans don't have whelps."

Han'zir just shrugs. "I guess we'll find out."

I look at their serious faces, baffled at the abrupt turn this has taken. But I'm not opposed to it. "You can try," I say, imagining myself carrying one of my own. Someday, when normalcy has returned, I think I would like that. "Good luck."

Han'zir clasps his hand into a fist and pumps it in the air, and Drazak answers by rolling his eyes.

That night, Drazak takes me first, feasting on me from head to toe, then clutching me close to his body as his cock urges me to open for him. "*Keva,* you feel perfect," he grunts. He teases my nipples and rubs my swollen clit until I'm gasping and clenching around him, and my skin is burning up. When he groans and releases everything inside me, there's so much that it drips out onto the blankets. As he rolls over, breathing heavily, Han'zir perches on top of me.

"I'm going to fuck all of him back into you," he says low in my ear. "And then I'm going to fill you, too, and make sure it all stays where it belongs." His cock is already thick and heavy, the soft head dripping his seed. He turns me over so my ass is in the air and slides inside me. I'm so slick with Drazak that there's an obscene, wet noise, and I clench around him at how delicious and desired this makes me feel.

"You're so tight, *keva,*" Han'zir moans, sinking in deep on his first thrust. I cry out as he fills me all the way full, so full that not all of him can fit, and Drazak's fluid spills down my legs. When our orc has recovered, he pours oil into his hand and runs his fingers between my ass cheeks while Han'zir desperately fucks me. When he arrives at the tight hole there, I whimper in anticipation.

"Drazak?" I ask, having never been touched there before. Drazak kisses the side of my face.

"Would you let me?" he asks. "It will feel good."

I nod hastily, wondering what he has planned. Will he take me the way that he takes Han'zir? He works his fingers inside me, opening me up, urging my body to give to him. I'm overcome by sheer sensation when one finally slips in, and almost immediately I reach my peak. I scream, every muscle in my body wrenching tight. With a groan, Han'zir shoves himself deep and unleashes inside me.

When we're finished, my thighs sticky with both of them, Drazak lifts my hips into his lap. He rubs a hand over my belly, and a hopeful smile spreads across his face.

"We'll try again and again," he murmurs, leaning his head down to rest between my breasts. "Until you're full with us."

I shudder all over, excited by this wild new idea they've had, and curious where it will lead when so many doors seem closed.

DRAZAK

After the incident with *whelp*, I decide I should try harder to teach Esme our language. There are lots of words she hasn't encountered yet that make it hard for her to tell us what she means.

And I want to know all of her. I want to hear everything she thinks, everything she longs to tell us. I want the three of us to have deep conversations around the fire for many nights. Already I've learned so many things about her: that she worked for a family, and took care of their children, and she lights up when she talks about them. I think she would be quite good with some of her own. But her enthusiasm quickly vanishes after that, and she falls quiet again. I sense there's more she isn't telling us.

When I'm not hunting or trying to fix up the old tiller to sell—not that anyone else has much coin left to buy it with—I'm drawing pictures of words I can think of, things that Esme might come across in her life. It's something to distract me when the nights start getting longer and the prospect of spending the winter without our usual stores of preserved goods looms larger.

I can't change it. If our new relationship has taught me anything, it's that there are some things in this world written about your life before you're ever born, and it's impossible to avoid them. All I can do is meet it head-on. I'll do as much to prepare as I can before the cold sets in, but there are many ugly, dark months ahead.

We'll have to make sacrifices. In a way, that steadies me, because I know that I would sacrifice anything for them so they don't have to feel the weight.

On a cool night, we gather around the fire, Esme sitting between my legs and Han'zir leaning half-asleep against my shoulder. I pull out the sheafs of paper where I've drawn of all sorts of things, from eggplant to butterfly to wagon wheel, and put one on the floor in front us.

"Butterfly," I tell Esme, gesturing at the drawing. She tilts her head, as if she doesn't quite comprehend.

"Drazak," Han'zir says in a solemn voice. "I hate to be the one to tell you, but you are not an artist."

"Shut up," I hiss at him, and clear my throat as I move the butterfly drawing away and replace it with the wheel.

About half of my drawings are passable, and Esme learns the words quickly. It entertains her, and she responds beautifully to my praise, her eyes pinching closed with how large she smiles.

"Cat," I tell her, gesturing at the drawing.

"Meow," she answers with a laugh. "Cat."

"And a kitten?" says Han'zir. He forms a tiny shape with his hands and makes a cute little kitten noise.

"Kitten," Esme answers, and I chuckle.

"Right." I flip the drawing over. "And this is a dog."

When she hears the word, Esme looks curiously down at it.

"Dog?" she repeats.

"Oh, and then it's you!" Han'zir says. He repeats the baby animal gesture. "A puppy!"

"Puppy?" she says, using her own name. The smile slowly falls from her face as she glances between us.

"A cute little puppy," Han'zir says brightly.

Her curiosity vanishes. My idiot troll doesn't notice the ghostly paleness that's fallen over her, the way her hands have stilled at her sides. Esme pulls away from me, snatching up the paper and holding it to her chest.

"Me?" she says, her voice trembling.

"Yes, silly." Han'zir reaches out to push some hair away from her eyes, but she slaps at his hand. He looks at me with confusion when she backs away from him.

"I'm your pet?" she asks in a hoarse whisper.

Ice fills my veins. "No, no," I tell her. "Esme. You're Esme, of course."

I scoot towards her on the floor, but again, Esme backs away. She shakes her head, fists clenched tight, and gets up to her feet.

"You have called me this since…" She searches for the word. "Since the beginning." Horror creeps across her face. "The first day. You called me this."

I follow her. "It was a nickname," Han'zir says in a calming voice. "Because you are—"

"Because I am your *dog*?!" Her words come out sharp and venomous. I didn't know she had this sort of anger in her, not until now. Her eyes are blazing, the whites turned red with unshed tears.

"You aren't," I tell her, taking her arm in my hand. "You aren't a dog. I promise." In response, she yanks it back.

"Then why you call me this?" The hurt in her eyes is unbearable. "You call me your dog. You keep me in the barn, and…" I can see how hard she's fighting not to cry.

"That was before," I say, hearing the desperation in my own voice.

"Before?" she says, keeping a greater and greater distance between us as I follow her away from the fire. "Before all of this? Before fucking me? Before telling me you—"

"Puppy," Han'zir says reflexively, "please."

It's like the blade of a sword has gone through her chest, the expression she makes.

"Whelps," she says, with a sort of sadness I've never heard before. "You want to use me. I am your toy."

"Esme. You're our mate." I try once more to stop her retreat, but instead, my reaching hand triggers something in her. Her entire body tenses, and that's when I know what she's going to do. "No!"

She takes off at a run, faster than I can blink, the paper flying into the air. Her legs move as quick as the wind, but immediately I'm running after her.

I can't let her go like this. I can't have her run from us.

But Esme's legs, while shorter, are also powerful, and her flight instinct is too strong. She races down the line of dying vegetable stalks and leaps over a fence like it's not there. I'm bigger, and I should be able to keep up with her—and catch her, like I absolutely must do, before she flees from here into enemy territory—but instead, I find myself falling behind as I climb over the fence, and her yellow dress weaves into the grass beyond the farm.

"Esme!" I shout, blazing after her through the meadow. She's headed straight for the trees.

She intends to lose me. She is not just upset. She is leaving us.

I call her name again, louder, trying to keep pace. She darts up the hill and then, I know that I've failed. She spends all her time foraging in these woods, and she can easily navigate them. Ahead of me, Esme slips between two trunks and vanishes into the darkened trees like a ghost.

"Please, Esme!" I'm gasping for air when I reach the top of the hill. It's dark enough now that I can't make out anything inside the tree cover. "Don't go!" I run headlong into the branches, but there's no sound ahead of me, not even her feet crunching leaves and twigs.

There's nothing but my own heavy breathing and my aching chest.

CHAPTER 13

K eva.

That's what they've been calling me, all along.

Their dog. Their little pet human. Their plaything. It feels like I'm being stabbed in the chest, over and over again.

Keva.

I'm deep in the woods now, and the sun set a while back. I remember the last time I slept in the forest, when I ran from the war. Nothing's really changed since then.

No, this hurts more. I was happy, for the first time in my life. I thought I had found something. I thought maybe I'd discovered my place in the world, between Drazak and Han'zir, my orc and my troll, and the farm was where I belonged. I thought that being with them was being home.

But it was some fucked up, twisted lie.

I slow down when I think I've finally lost Drazak. The despair soon morphs into fury as I think of him, of how I *knew* him, the very first moment I saw him. How he seemed so familiar to me.

Perhaps he's broken my heart before.

And Han'zir. My troll, out of everyone, has only ever seen me as an animal to do his bidding and warm his bed. All those pats on the head... remembering it makes me seethe in a place I've never felt before.

He was the one who gave me that name.

Back at the mansion on the hill, I was a toy to my master, something to pick on when he couldn't use his wife or children, something to hit and scream at when his own boiling rage got to be too much. I was an object to bear his suffering.

You useless cow.

I did everything for him and his family, and I was little more than a piece of furniture to them.

Then I became a pawn in an even bigger game, a chunk of flesh to be thrown at the enemy, meant to stop the tide of arrows and swords and gunfire.

I will not be someone's plaything again. I will not be used as a pet, as a body, as a womb.

Finally, at last, I cry. I fall into the forest floor and drop my head to the dirt, slamming my fist into it over and over.

Rather than trying to get up and continue on, I roll onto my side in the needles and branches. This time I do manage to sleep, because it's the only way to escape how they've betrayed me.

Han'zir

She's gone. I know it before I even see Drazak approaching in the darkness hours later. I went after them, but I was no match for my orc or my girl.

Her soul has left us.

He doesn't speak as he comes back and sits down on a log.

"We should search for her," I say.

"I did." He pokes at the fire. "She's gone, Han. And she's not coming back."

My throat closes. That isn't right. "She'll be back tomorrow," I say, whether to convince him or myself, I'm not sure.

"You saw her face." He hunches even further forward. "Something broke her. *We* broke her."

I drop my head in my hands. *Puppy.* What a horrible thing, I think now, to have called her. My disgust at myself rises up over me like a monster, eclipsing everything else.

Now we've lost her, the third point in our constellation. I wonder what will happen to us without her—and what will happen to *her* without us.

Our bed feels cold, and though I try to find Drazak's hand, he curls it into a fist and pulls it away. I know he's not angry at me. He's angry at himself, at *us*, for not realizing how cruel we were.

The next day, she doesn't come back.

The farm looks dead. The sky is a tepid gray, and neither of us speak as we do what few chores we can. When I stoop down to weed, I can almost imagine Esme next to me, and I fall back on my heels.

She's far from her own lands out there. She has no weapons, no food, no means of survival. Where will she go next?

I doubt she had a plan when she left. No, she was acting out of panic, hurt, anger. I didn't know she had the capacity for so much rage.

There had been a fear in her eyes, too—something beyond just nicknames, that had fueled her legs. She was fleeing from us the way a deer might flee from a bear.

I'm consumed with the thought of what might happen to her. My Esme. My gentle, happy girl. She was our sun, warming up the sky, keeping the clouds away.

By afternoon, I can't think of anything but her being found by soldiers and cut down like wheat. I find Drazak once again trying to fix something, but he's doing more harm than good.

"We have to go look for her," I say, standing over his shoulder.

"She's gone, Han." He doesn't even look up. "We won't find her."

"So you're going to give up on trying?" I demand. He pauses what he's doing and his ear twitches, but otherwise he doesn't answer me. "You're going to leave her out there to die?"

His shoulders tense. "What else can I do? She wanted to go. I tried to stop her. But I can't make her come back." He turns the wrench roughly. "I can't force her to love us again."

The words burn.

"I just want the chance to convince her," I say, my voice rising. "That's all. She was scared. Now she's out there alone. If we could find her, I know she'd come back."

When Drazak turns to me, the only emotion on his face is despair.

"She already has a day on us," he says, and it comes out hoarse. "We'll never catch up to her. We have no way of knowing which way she went."

How can he give up when she's done so much for us, when she's a part of us?

"Fine." I turn around and head back home. "I'm going. You can stay."

Drazak's on his feet in a second. "You can't be serious. You'll be looking for days, or weeks. What about the war? There are humans out there, too. Soldiers everywhere."

But right now, I don't give a fuck who's out there besides our Esme. I will do whatever I have to do to get her back, even if I do it alone.

Leaving Drazak there, I head into the kitchen and start packing my bag. I bring what rations we can possibly spare, not knowing how long I'll be gone. The door flies open and Drazak comes in, putting both hands on my shoulders.

"This is a bad idea—" he begins.

I shake him off and grab my bag, heading for the door. "I don't care what you think." My gaze levels on him. "I have to find her. That's what she means to me. It's what I would do for you, too. What *she* would do for you."

He flinches. I can tell then, by the look in his eyes, that he is a husk without a will to fight, a shell of himself without Esme here to be his heart, too.

"You shouldn't go alone," he grumbles. I stand by the fire pit as he pulls out a bag and stuffs it full with the rest of our food, everything left in the house, then heads to the door. "You coming?" he asks.

Drazak doesn't intend to come back. If we're going to do this, we're going all-in.

ESME

Drazak doesn't find me that night, but at first dawn, I start moving again in case he and Han'zir come looking for me. The hurt and the rage drive me deeper into the woods.

I manage to find a few things to eat along the way, stopping at a big thicket of blackberry bushes to fill my aching stomach. Where am I going? So far I haven't encountered any trollkin, but surely my luck will run out soon. I wonder how the war's gone since I left the front lines. Did that redheaded woman make it out alive?

Do whatever you have to do to survive.

That was the first time anyone had suggested to me that trollkin weren't too different from us. Now I think that's true. They're just as capable of being manipulative bastards as humans are.

My legs are getting tired. I'll need to rest again soon, and hope that eventually I find someplace safe, somewhere far from this war. I don't know how long I'll need to walk, but I'll keep going as long as I have to, even if it means crossing mountains.

Then, up ahead, I hear voices. Horses. I almost don't recognize my own language at first because it's been so long since I spoke it. They're coming towards me quickly, and I know what they are before they even appear.

Soldiers.

"Hey!" a voice shouts. They've seen me already. I dart away into the trees, knowing exactly what will happen if they get their hands on me. I saw it once, when a man caught deserting was driven straight through by a sword. At the time I'd thought it was foolish to kill a soldier in the middle of a war, where every body was useful. Now I understand that it was a warning to the rest of us.

"Catch her!" Another voice comes from my left. I push my legs harder, thinking of the master right on my heels, screeching "Bitch!" at the top of his lungs. If I'm caught, I will face a far worse punishment.

More hoofbeats, this time in front of me. I stop and turn on my heel, heading off to my right. But in that direction there are even more voices. "Fan out! Find her!"

I have to go back. They won't expect me to go back. I spin again and take off, running the way I came.

A shot rings out, striking a tree right near my head. Stepping out of the trees is a familiar woman on a massive brown horse, her gun pointed at me. It's spent, so she draws her sword.

"Don't move," she growls, sliding out of her saddle. I turn to run again, but more horses are already there, surrounding me. The other soldiers dismount, too, and soon there are swords pointed at me from five different directions.

"Deserter," one of them mutters.

"We'll take her back to town," the woman says. "String her up in the square for everyone to see. They'll understand what becomes of deserters."

I don't fight when one of the soldiers approaches me and ties a rope around my wrists. There's no point.

I won't escape my fate this time.

Chapter 14

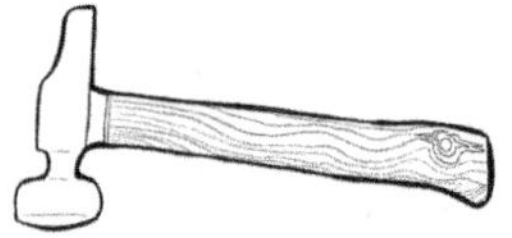

DRAZAK

It's not like there's anything left for us at the farm anyway. All that lies in front of us are dead ends.

But Han'zir is right. We have to get her back. Without her, there's an emptiness in my soul, a gaping hole where Esme should be.

We both know that going after her means venturing into human territory. That's where she'd have gone, surely—back to her own kind. It will make our task that much more dangerous.

We've brought along what weapons we can. I have a bow and an axe, and Han'zir's strapped his spear over his back with a knife in a sheath. Perhaps if we only come across a few humans at a time, we stand a chance.

We both know we can't return without our mate or we'll never be whole again.

I have a rough idea of where the lines are drawn since the humans started occupying trollkin towns. Once we get there, of course, who knows where she'll be. This is probably a fool's errand that'll get us killed, but the alternative is to always wonder what became of Esme, to live the rest of our lives missing an important piece of ourselves. When she dies, we'll go with her.

Han'zir and I walk for most of the day before stopping to eat, where we try to take as little as possible from our store of rations. We gather what we can along the way, but all the berry bushes we pass have been picked over.

This is a good sign. Perhaps Esme went this way. That's my hope, and I'll cling to it as long as I can.

My chest aches as I remember the look on her face when she learned the truth. Something inside her took over at that moment, some kind of deep pain that Han'zir and I aren't privy to.

Suddenly, he stops in front of me and I almost bump into him.

"I can feel something," he says quietly. "I think we might be getting closer."

"What?" I frown. "How could you possibly know?"

He just shrugs. "I can sense it. The longer we've headed this direction, the stronger the feeling gets. I think we're on the right track."

All I can do is hope he's right. Han'zir has always had a deeper intuition than I do.

"Lead the way," I tell him, hiking my bag up higher on my shoulder. If it means we can find her, I'm all ears.

I will walk to the ends of the earth if it means we can have her back.

ESME

They don't even put me on a horse. After tying the rope around my hands, I'm forced to trot along behind the procession of soldiers as they lead me back to town, where I'll finally meet the end I was always intended for.

I should've stayed when we charged into battle against the trollkin. I should've been there alongside my comrades as they tried to take the town. Maybe I would've found that redheaded woman and lived. Maybe I could've gotten out of all this and someday gone home.

Home? Home to the mansion on the hill and the master who tormented me? After all this, I know one thing: I am not an object to be used. I make my own choices. Maybe some of those are poor choices, but at least I'm the one who decides them.

When we reach town, my legs are jelly and my breath comes ragged. The woman on the big brown horse dismounts, and a squirrelly, skinny man joins us.

"Colonel," he says, ducking his head with respect. "Who's this?"

"Deserter." She snatches up my rope and pulls me in, her sharp eyes boring into me. I resist the urge to shrink back at the fury in them. "We should hang her. Bring in every squadron, especially those new recruits, and make them watch."

The stick-like man nods again deferentially. "Of course, of course. She would make a great example of what happens to people who run from the King's call." Then his shoulders tighten and he wrings his hands. "However... we do rather need all the bodies we can get."

The colonel's eyes snap to him. "Are you arguing with me?"

He pales and waves a hand. "No, no. Not at all. I'm merely suggesting that we could use her instead of breaking her neck. She's young and strong, and now that we've commandeered all the production capacity, we're in need of individuals who can, erm, work the land."

Commandeered? Does that mean they've stolen the trollkin farms and taken over? I think of Drazak and Han'zir, simply living their lives when humans arrive to take the rest of it, and my blood turns cold.

But this is, potentially, an opportunity to escape death, if this twig of a man can convince my captor not to break my neck.

"I'm familiar with trollkin farm equipment," I say suddenly, and the colonel glares at me.

"Keep your mouth shut. You have no say in this, deserter."

But the man's eyes are curious now. "Really. I was... indentured on a trollkin farm for the last few months. I know how everything works—"

"Silence!" The colonel yanks on my rope, dragging me towards her until we're face-to-face. "No one asked you. Now shut up."

But I've caught the man's attention. He peers at me, studying me to see if I might be lying.

"The tillers," I say, thinking of Drazak asking me to hand him different tools as he repaired one. "They don't work like ours. The trollkin have a totally different method for tilling."

There's a growl low in the colonel's throat, but the stick-man holds up a hand to her. "We've been having trouble with this," he tells her, then gestures at me. "We've had to do everything by hand."

The colonel's brows furrow in thought. "Is this the hold-up we've been facing with planting?" she asks, never once taking her razor-sharp eyes off of mine.

"One of them."

"I can help," I interject. "I also know what all their vegetables need. You're probably overwatering those big roots, the white ones. They actually like it very dry."

The colonel is about to strangle me for speaking out of turn when the skinny man steps in. "If it's all the same to you, colonel," he says, gingerly reaching for the rope, "I think we could use this one." When she opens her mouth to object, he adds, "It's still servitude. She'll spend the rest of her life working herself to the bone, without pay, to serve and further the mission. Perhaps that's a fate even worse than death."

I don't really agree with him, but I nod hastily anyway. The colonel thinks, looking me over from head to toe.

"She's a good age, and she looks tough. I wonder what else she's learned that could be useful to us?" Her frown morphs into a wicked smile. "What else we could do to take out more trollkin?"

Again I think of my orc and my troll, the humans charging in and cutting them down to take the farm. Then I shake my head. They're not mine, not like I thought they were. Still, a deeply-buried hole inside me aches. It is cavernous, absorbing all the light around it, and I don't think it will ever be filled again.

The colonel hands off my rope. "Make sure to put her at the bottom of the food chain," she says. "Treat her like the animal she is, leaving her own fellow soldiers to die."

I want to argue, *none of us should have been out there in the first place*, but she could always change her mind about the gallows.

The squirrely man nods a few times eagerly. "I know just where to take her. And I'll find out everything we can about how the trollkin are surviving the war."

Begrudgingly, the colonel nods and releases the rope. I can only hope that what they have planned for me isn't worse than death.

Once again, I'm a thing, a bargaining chip, a tool to be used until I break and serve no other purpose.

This time I'm put on a horse, though my hands are still tied. The skinny man is some kind of magistrate. He oversees transporting me to the farm where I'll be stationed and made to work.

There's an irony there that doesn't escape me.

"You're going to show me everything," he says, adjusting the collar of his shirt. "Then I'll write a guide, and then the Colonel will see."

I nod along as we march down a long dirt road. Up in the distance there's a big barn that looks much like the one on our own farm. They've left the animals alive, which perhaps makes them an inch smarter than the trollkin who came and took everything.

We're greeted by an overseer, a growly man who's short and square and reminds me the tiniest bit of Drazak. He doesn't need to be tall to be intimidating.

"What's this?" the overseer asks, arms crossed. "More hands? It won't do us much good unless—"

"She will solve your problem," the skinny man announces, passing him my rope. "She worked on a trollkin farm and claims she can operate the equipment."

The overseer turns to me, surveying me carefully.

"Interesting." He tugs on my rope. "Let's see, then."

I'm shown to one of the tillers, which these idiots can't figure out how to use. I explain the method that Drazak taught me once upon a time and show them how to attach the tiller to a horse.

"We've been using it all wrong," the skinny man says, taking copious notes.

The overseer nods in approval. "We can get started right now. There are plenty of winter crops we can plant."

In a way, I feel as if I'm betraying Drazak and Han'zir by giving out this information. Who knows who lived on this farm before the humans came? But this is what I have to do now to survive.

When night comes, I'm tied to a pole in the barn and left to sleep in the dirt, with only a lantern to cast any light. The overseer's dog, a big black creature with white and brown markings, lies down next to me and curls against my side. I can't help thinking of my hayloft and the time Han'zir slept with me there, bundling me up tight in his arms.

CHAPTER 15

Han'zir

I can feel her somewhere out there. Almost see her, like a candle flickering in a far-off window. The closer we get to her, the faster my heart beats, guiding me steadily in her direction.

I'd always dreamed of finding the mating bond and meeting someone meant for me. My parents didn't have it, but my uncle did. I knew whenever I saw him with her that it was out there for me, too, but I never thought I'd find it this way. As much as it hurts to remember how Esme ran from us, I also remember the joy of the three of us being together. And oh, how pure and good that joy was. I close my eyes and think of her face smiling, her lashes fluttering as she fell asleep in Drazak's arms, how it felt to be buried inside her and clutching her close to my chest. How every time I watched Drazak's glorious cock slide in and out of her, watched her laugh or make that cute little frowning face when she concentrated, I felt like I was exactly where I was supposed to be.

I cling onto this, using it to guide me to her. Where it leads, I don't know, but I have to hope that she wasn't brought to us, our truth shown to us, just to have her taken away.

It's ominous walking down trollkin roads and past abandoned trollkin homes. We're deep in occupied territory now, but have gotten lucky enough not to run across any human soldiers. We found one man, wearing a badge much like our Esme had been when we first found her, running for his life.

We let him go. He was very grateful.

On our third day, though, we come across the first farm. We're about to stroll through and search for spoiled food when we hear voices. Drazak seizes me by the arm and we duck behind a patch of brambles.

Humans. They're in the fields, harvesting our crops, making a mess of them. Equipment sits abandoned, some of it disassembled.

"Shit," growls Drazak. "Is this where she is, Han?"

I shake my head. The flickering light I'm certain is our Esme is still farther on. Drazak grunts in annoyance.

"We're going to have to stay here then, until dark. We can't be seen." This is empty farmland, certainly no woods to hide in.

So, we make camp and wait. In the meantime, I study the humans going about their business. It's embarrassing, really, watching them puzzle over the equipment. And they're harvesting the tubers much too early.

I drift off while we wait, but Drazak remains steadfastly sitting, staring off into nothing.

"What are you thinking about?" I ask as the sun starts to dip below the horizon, and the humans retreat indoors for their meal.

"I'm trying to find her," Drazak says, his eyes never leaving the patch of sky he's been focused on. "I want to feel her like you can."

I put a hand on his shoulder. "We're connected to different parts of her, in different ways," I say. "It doesn't mean you're any less of a mate."

He sighs and leans back, finally looking at me. "If we manage to find her, what do we do? How do we convince her to come home to us?"

I shake my head. "We'll have to figure it out when we get there."

When the sun has gone down and it looks like the humans have retired for the night, we start across the field, hoping no one catches sight of two trollkin wandering through the darkness.

Esme

As promised, they put me to work.

First, I set up the tiller like Drazak always did. When his face appears in my mind, I think of the way his tusks brushed his cheeks when I earned a rare smile, and my fury and misery whirl up together into a tornado. Then I'm tasked with tilling the field. I work all day, sweating despite the cool fall air. I think of Han'zir, following along behind the tiller, gently planting each seed and whispering something to it as he covers it with dirt. By the time evening comes around, my body is ready to give out underneath me, and when dinner is served, I get the smallest portion of rations.

"The Colonel takes everything else," the overseer says with a begrudging grunt. "You get the scraps, girl."

I accept what I can and wolf it down without thinking of saving any for later. There's always someone watching me in the daylight, and at night I'm tied up once more and left in the barn to rot. It's hard not to think of the big bed in the low clay house with the pulled leather roof, how it felt to sleep there curled up against my orc's big shoulder, with my troll's arm slung over my waist. It's painful in so many ways, thinking of what I lost, how they both used me.

Every night, the dog lies down next to me, like she knows I'm all alone.

This will be every day from now until the rest of time, I realize. Shackled to a post, sleeping in the dirt next to the dog I've nicknamed Keva, thinking of home. The two holes inside me ache and fester, and I wonder what happened on the farm, how I was tied so closely to Han'zir and Drazak that being without them makes me famished deep in my heart.

I've been there for who knows how many days, working myself to the bone from sunrise to sunset and eating bits of leftover ham and rotting greens, when there's a commotion by the big house. Something is happening.

The overseer and I both run to find out what the ruckus is about. It's the colonel again, this time flanked by soldiers with horses and carts. It all looks very familiar.

"She's here," the overseer hisses. He heads towards the colonel and dips his head in respect. I stay put. I would never try to escape surrounded by soldiers, not unless I wanted to actually be hanged this time.

"What brings you visiting today?" asks the overseer. The colonel dismounts her horse.

"Supplies. Rations." She gestures over her shoulder, and the soldiers bring the wagons into the field. They head for the grain silo first to take what they want. The overseer's hands clench into fists as he silently watches them head to the storage shed, retrieving crate after crate of produce. They load up the wagons while the colonel surveys the farm, checking inside the house for anything else the workers might have squirreled away.

I feel empty as I watch it happen again. How many will go hungry so we can continue to invade trollkin land? Once again, I face a winter of starvation so the bloodshed can go on. I'm no better off here than I was with Drazak and Han'zir. At least there I had my orc and my troll. At least there I slept in a soft bed.

I can't think like that. That life is gone for me now. The last of my hope drains out of me as the wagons are filled, and the soldiers haul them away, all of our supplies going with them.

"Colonel," the overseer says, a hint of desperation in his voice. "If you take everything, we'll have nothing to eat. And we can't work the land without something to eat."

She shrugs, disaffected. "We all have to make sacrifices for the cause."

I grind my teeth. There are monsters on both sides of this war.

The overseer grumbles and gestures at one of the women working to clean up after the soldiers. "Take her to the barn," he snaps, and points at me. Then he turns back to the soldiers who are pulling harvests off the plants, as if disbelieving what's in front of him.

"This is how it always goes," I tell him as the woman wraps a rope around my wrists. "On both sides."

He turns around and slaps me across the face, and it echoes in my ears. Then I'm dragged away.

DRAZAK

The sensation of *home* is getting stronger. The longer we walk through the night, the more I feel like we're somewhere familiar. It's the way I felt the first time I looked into Esme's eyes, when I recognized her from some other lifetime.

Perhaps this is it, my connection with her, the way Han'zir has his. The sensation of rightness, like every step is taking me closer to the place where I'm supposed to be.

As the sun starts to rise, we find an abandoned outbuilding to hide in during the day. We'll try to get some shut-eye, and then keep going once the sun sets again.

I've already lost track of the days. It all feels endless without our third star.

Han'zir takes off his cloak and spreads it out under us, then wraps his big body around mine. His hand finds its way down from my chest to my groin, easily unlacing the front of my trousers, where my cock is waiting for him. In the darkness, he strokes me slowly, waiting with a quiet patience as it thickens in his palm. He plays with me just the way I like while he kisses my throat, then nibbles on my ear. When I finally go off in his hand, it's not powerful, but it's soothing in a way that I needed.

My troll, who knows me inside and out.

We fall asleep that way, his arms curled around me, our backs and shoulders sore from the hard ground.

We're awoken by the sound of barks. I'm on my feet instantly, hatchet in hand. Have they finally found us?

Han'zir's right behind me as I open the rickety door. On the other side is a rather large dog, mostly black with spots of brown and white. It's barking wildly at us, but it doesn't seem angry, wagging its tail. When we emerge from the building and look around, there don't seem to be any humans in sight.

"What are you doing here?" I ask, as if the dog could reply. Instead, it leaps up, frantically licking any part of me it can reach. I shove it away.

Han'zir has a quizzical look on his face. "Where'd a dog come from?" he asks, peering around.

I shrug. "Who knows. Maybe it's loose." My belly feels sour just looking at it. It reminds me of everything we had and everything we lost.

When the greeting is over with, the dog trots away from us,

still wagging. When we don't move, it stops and runs back, barking again.

Han'zir and I exchange a glance. It can't really be trying to tell us something, can it? But the sun is only just starting to set, and anyone could see us if we went gallivanting around.

"It's still daylight," I grunt. "We shouldn't be out here." Once more the dog runs on ahead, then turns and barks at us. I've never believed in things like signs before, but if there ever was one...

"I think we should go with it," Han'zir says. He nods towards the dog. "It's not like we've had any luck on our own so far."

I have to agree. We've simply been following our guts, and still we haven't found Esme. We have to take the chance.

The dog happily leads us away from the abandoned farm, through the tall grasses. We keep low as we follow, past a silent, dark farmhouse and a big empty field, stripped bare by the humans. We follow the white tip at the end of the creature's tail until the sound of raised voices drifts towards us.

There's nowhere to hide out here, so I grab Han'zir's shoulder and duck close to the ground, hoping they won't see us in the dim light. The dog circles us a few times, but thankfully, doesn't make a sound. When the arguing finally stops, it's full dark.

"I think she's here," Han'zir breathes. He turns to me with glittering eyes. "She's here, Drazak."

I glance down at the dog, who's made itself comfortable at our feet. Everything has been guiding us towards her, and now we just have one last leg of the journey to go.

"But where?" I ask, gesturing at the sprawling farm. "She could be inside the house, or—"

As if on cue, the dog hops to its feet, ears pricking forward.

"Keva?" a small voice calls out. The dog's tail wags madly, and it takes off towards the barn. Han'zir and I exchange a look, then I get up and jog after it. If we get caught now, we get caught. This is the final gambit.

The dog vanishes inside the barn. I walk close to the wall, making sure to stay in the shadows, Han'zir following close behind.

"Aw, Keva." I hear a familiar sad sigh, and Esme says something else in her language I don't understand.

She's here. She's really here. I know the sound of her voice in my body, in my soul. With a swift glance around to make sure we're alone, I gesture at Han'zir to follow me. His expression is giddy, all smiles. But we're not out of the woods yet.

We still have to convince her to come home with us—and then get there safely.

ESME

Keva rushes into the barn, tail wagging, and feverishly licks my face.

"What's gotten into you?" I ask her. They've tied me up while the Colonel and the overseer argue inside the house. Keva runs to the open barn doors, still wagging, and barks.

"Shh!" comes a voice from the other side. I sit up against the post.

"Who's there?" I call out. I'm helpless here, tied up like I am. I couldn't get away if someone came for me.

A huge shadow appears in the doorway—no, two of them. I shrink back against the post.

"Esme?" I recognize Drazak's voice. When the figure ducks inside, the lamplight illuminates his face.

My orc. And behind him, my troll. My heart surges to the surface, crying out for them, screaming their names. But it's a damaged, whimpering cry, cut and bruised. The tears I've been holding in since the colonel found me leak out as Drazak kneels down in front of me. He's wearing a heavy pack, his bow and quiver over his shoulder, his face dirty. Just like I remember him.

"What are you doing here?" I ask in a hoarse whisper. "Why did you come?"

Han'zir drops into the dirt next to me. "I'm so sorry," he says, reaching out to touch me, and then stopping himself.

If the colonel discovers them here... I shudder. "How did you find me?" I hiss. Keva barks again, as if announcing her presence. I shush her. The farm is crawling with other humans, and I can't have her drawing their attention now.

"The dog," Drazak says quietly. "We need to get you out of here." He reaches for my ropes and tries to untangle them.

The voices outside draw closer. The colonel is touring the farm looking for any last scraps of food the overseer might have hidden away.

"She's coming," I whisper at them. While I'm distracted, Han'zir slices the ropes through in one motion.

"Who?" Drazak asks, urging me to stand up.

"Bad person." I shake my head and point at the door. "You have to go."

Drazak scowls. "We're not leaving without you."

I glance at them and the ropes we left behind. Outside, the colonel is talking louder and louder about insubordination, and how the King treats disobedience.

"I can't go with you." I won't exchange one servitude for another, as much as my heart aches and burns for them. They can hurt me in a deeper, different way than the colonel can. "Leave."

Drazak's heavy lower lip turns down even further. "No."

"Leave!" I whisper it louder this time. "You have to go, now. Before they find you." But how will two trollkin possibly escape the farm alive while it's crawling with soldiers?

Han'zir glances up at the lantern hanging overhead, and grins.

"I have an idea." He snatches it off the hook, and with a glance at us, says, "We'd better run."

Nodding in understanding, Drazak picks me up around the middle and tosses me over his shoulder like a bag of potatoes. I resist shouting at him, but I bang on his back with my fists. He's so bulky and muscular it makes no difference.

Han'zir breaks the glass and hurls the lantern into the straw. It catches fire instantly, and within moments, the flames are spreading to the walls.

Carrying me like a limp fish, Drazak races out the barn doors, Han'zir close behind. The flames shoot up the dry wood beams, crackling as they travel to the roof.

"Keva!" I call out. The dog appears, ears flattened to her head at the smell of smoke. The air fills with shouts and screams as the fire arcs up into the sky above the barn. Drazak sticks to the building's shadow as we creep around it, the dog in tow, and I can feel the heat of the flames on my skin. People are fetching water as the fire spreads. All the animals that lived here have already been slaughtered, but the barn is close to the house, and the sparks could easily jump.

When we reach the edge of the barn, Drazak pauses. "We're going to have to run," he says to me. He drops me to the ground, grabs my hand, and looks into my eyes. "Please, Esme. Will you run?"

My soul knows I have to go with him. So we run.

But we've only gotten a few yards from the barn when I hear thundering hoofbeats. A huge, familiar brown horse gallops in front of us, blocking our way—and riding it is the Colonel, her gun aimed at my face.

"Don't move," she snarls. All three of us freeze. "I knew there was something strange about you. Your story didn't add up." She gestures at Drazak and Han'zir with the barrel of the gun. "Move, and I'll shoot them. That'll be two pairs of tusks for my mantelpiece."

I glance between my orc and my troll. They can't die, not here, not now.

So I don't budge. The Colonel snarls in fury. "Overseer!" she shouts. "We have a runaway!"

Like the rest of the humans, though, the big oaf is busy dumping water on the fire, while the others build a barricade to the house.

"So what?" he shouts back. "We have bigger problems!"

The Colonel turns the barrel of her gun on him. Without any warning she presses the trigger, and the overseer screams as the bullet punctures his shoulder. She turns back to us, drawing her sword.

"I will cut you down, traitor," she says, dismounting her horse, sword still pointed at us. "But first I will torture you, little girl, and find out everything you know."

Damn it. I wish Han'zir and Drazak hadn't come for me. Next to me, Keva growls.

"Let us go, and deal with what's important," I snap at the colonel. "You can't pillage this farm for food if there's nothing left of it."

But she simply laughs at me. "You think I care about one little farm?" Then she lunges towards Drazak, her sword outstretched. Before she can reach him...

A massive wooden spear flies through the air, gliding right through her throat.

The Colonel gurgles, blood bubbling out of the wound, and she stumbles forward. Drazak and I back away as she falls to the ground, spilling red across the dirt. Han'zir walks towards her and yanks his spear out of her limp body, shooting me a wide smile.

"We'll always protect you," he says. And I know it's true.

But the overseer is running over to us with his gun ready, his own wound drizzling hot blood. Drazak raises his hand axe, and Han'zir holds the spear over his shoulder, ready to hurl it again. But the gun would land its killing blow first.

The man stops cold when he sees what Han'zir's done. "You killed her," he says, glancing between us and the colonel's body, his face going slack.

I can't let him shoot one of my trollkin. "Step aside and let us go," I say.

He raises the gun so it's aimed at me. Drazak snarls, but I hold out a hand to stop him.

"So that's how you knew." The overseer shakes his head. "Indentured servant my ass." His gun hand shakes, his other arm bleeding profusely from his bullet wound.

Then, the faintest smile flickers across his face. He lowers the gun and takes a few steps back. "You took care of our biggest problem for us," he says, kicking the colonel. "I have to give you credit for that."

I exhale with relief. Then I tug on Han'zir and Drazak's hands. "We have to go," I say in Trollkin. They both nod at me, and we take off running into the grass, with Keva close behind. The overseer doesn't follow us as the barn is consumed by the fire.

HAN'ZIR

It worked.

I can't believe we got out alive, but our Esme is as smart as she is sweet. And we've apparently obtained a new member of our family.

The dog happily follows us as we leave the farm behind. None of the humans do. They had no problem letting her go after treating her as an object to be kept in a barn and tied up with rope.

But Esme is worth so much more than that, and I'll make sure she knows it for as long as I'm alive.

When we're a safe distance away, we stop to untie the twine around her hands, and I find red marks where it bit into her flesh. I rub them, but she yanks them away.

"Why did you come?" she asks, voice low and angry. "I left you. I don't belong to you."

I crouch down in front of her so I can look straight into her eyes. "You could run to the end of the world and we would follow you," I say, pouring all of my misery over the last week into the words, all of the yearning deep in my body to have her back. "You are our mate, Esme. Our star. We cannot live without you."

Her lip trembles. There is so much hurt buried inside her that I wish I could dig out and banish.

"I'm sorry for what we did," Drazak says, taking one of her small hands in his big one. He weaves their fingers together, and though she tenses up, she doesn't pull away. "I'm so sorry. You're our everything. I'll do whatever I have to do to make it up to you."

Tears dribble from the corners of her eyes. There is more to her hurt than simply a nickname. Something deep and buried is clawing at her insides.

"I can't be your pet." Her shoulders curl, like she's protecting herself. "My master... I was his dog, too." When she looks at us again, there is a fire in her eyes. "I will not be this. Not again. Not even for you."

All I want is to embrace our Esme, to show her what she means to me, but I have to earn that from her again.

"You are anything but a pet." Drazak brings her hand to his chest. "You are my heart. Without you, I'm not myself. Neither of us are."

I put my hand over theirs, cradling her between us. "I want everything that is you, Esme. I want all your thoughts and dreams and fears. I want to give you the home and the life you've always deserved, where you are *you*."

Her big eyes swallow these words. When I reach out to brush her cheek, she doesn't move away, and I draw her into my arms. There she starts to cry, her face pressed into my neck, still holding Drazak's hand.

"I've missed you," I say, stroking her hair, relishing simply in the feeling of her body against mine. "More than life itself."

When I release her, Drazak sweeps her up, lifting her off the ground as he embraces her. The dog barks in excitement as he kisses her, deeply and thoroughly, and her legs wrap around his hips. They're both panting when he finally sets her down, and it's as if the air is electrified.

"Will you come home with us?" he asks her. "Will you be our partner, our equal in everything for as long as we live?"

She hiccups, tears streaming even faster down her face. For a moment I fear she'll turn us away, that the injury runs too deep to overcome. Then, slowly, she nods. I wipe the tears away and kiss her cheek, then her nose, then her lips. She sinks into me, and I've never felt such relief, such happiness as having her with us again.

"Yes." Esme sniffles. "Take me home, please." The dog furiously licks her hand, and she giggles. "And little Keva here."

I glance up at Drazak with chagrin. "You got that dog you wanted."

His smile brings his tusks all the way up to his eyes. "I have everything," he says with a nod. "Everything I could ever want."

DRAZAK

We are still presented with the problem of escaping human territory alive. But we managed to find Esme here, and we can get out the same way.

My body thirsts for our human's, but I will just have to wait. I need to earn her trust back, her love. And yet as she walks between us, the dog leading the way, my cock is straining my breeches. I want nothing more than to show her what she means to me, how my very being desires to be reunited with her again, to feel the strength of our bond return.

Han'zir rubs my shoulder. "Soon," he whispers in my ear, making the hair on my neck stand on end.

Once again we travel by night, crossing field after field, until we reach the safety of the dense woods. We keep our weapons at the ready in case we run into soldiers. It seems, though, that they're occupied elsewhere. Smoke rises into the sky in the distance, and I can almost smell the burnt flesh.

When we meet two scouts in the woods, we spot them before they spot us. I ready an arrow and let it fly, striking the first one in the head. As he falls from his horse, Han'zir leaps out with his spear and hurls it through the second soldier. Esme gasps and covers her mouth, watching as both of them tumble to the forest floor. I fear that seeing her kinsmen killed in front of her will send her running, but instead she approaches their horses, her eyes wide.

"New horses!" She climbs up on one, and I get up behind her. Han'zir takes the other, Keva following happily behind us.

We stop to bathe in a river on the way, and seeing our Esme's soft body again, I can't keep myself from touching her. Though she has kept a tight hold on her affections until now, she relaxes into my hands, and I see my need reflected back at me in her eyes. I can't help myself any longer, and my fingers find their way to her peaked nipples, then to the warm, soft place between her legs. Han'zir approaches her from behind, his cock just as swollen and hard as mine. She moans as it slips between her cheeks, and Han'zir's eyes roll back in his head.

"Please," Esme says quietly, stroking my chest, her hand trailing down my belly to my straining, heavy cock. "Please, Drazak."

And so, while she lies back in Han'zir's arms, I take her. Being inside her soft, tight cunt again is like being home. I'm so overwhelmed by the sensation of her, her tiny lips on mine, that I crest far too soon. Remembering how she left us, I pull out and empty myself into the river.

"My turn," Han'zir says, bringing her into his lap. She rises up over his cock, and my hands holding her up, she slides down onto it. He groans, and the sound of him slicking in and out of her makes me thick all over again. Esme reaches for me, and when she takes me into her hot, wet mouth, I'm enraptured. She sucks on me, moaning as she rises up and down on Han'zir's lap, taking both of us into her perfect body. The sound of their pleasure easily brings me to my powerful finish, and Esme's eyes go wide as I fill up her mouth. Han'zir pulls himself free at the last moment, his seed spraying across her.

"I suppose we'll need to wash you again," I say, sweeping some away from her well-loved lips. She grabs my hand and licks it up, and I think that I might be the luckiest damn orc that ever did live.

Keva hurls herself into the river alongside us, and watching Esme play with her, I know that we are finally all together—that our circle is complete.

Chapter 17

To be with my troll and my orc again, there is nothing like it. I have no words to describe how it feels to sleep between them again, even on the hard forest floor. We make our way across occupied territory, staying as far as we can from the sounds of battle.

By coming for me, they've made it clear to me who I am to them.

And then, the trees end and the valley spreads out below us, and I can't help but run towards it—back to my home. Keva barks and runs alongside me, and I hear Han'zir call my name. They follow on our new horses, who will help us till the fields and restore the farm again.

Though there is very little food left, and the cold air tastes of the upcoming winter, hope blooms in my chest. If we survived this, we can survive anything.

First thing in the morning, Drazak slings his bow over his back and leaves into the woods to search for something to eat. Han'zir, Keva and I forage for what we can find, and I'm glad to discover mushrooms are in season. Han'zir knows which ones are safe and which aren't, and we return from our first day with two heavy baskets full of soft, meaty mushrooms to eat.

Drazak manages to land a young deer, and it will provide sustenance for two weeks at least. The winter crops we planted are starting to sprout, and I'm optimistic that we'll make it through.

Of course we will, as long as we have each other.

But it's a difficult winter. The food runs low and game is scarce, and there are some nights we go hungry. Keva is adept at catching rabbits, though, and keeps herself fed.

It isn't long before the dog starts to get bigger and more sluggish. "I think she's going to have puppies," Han'zir says. He's become very fond of her, and Drazak always watches him cuddle her in front of the fire with a sly grin.

The cold nights are not so bad with my troll and my orc to keep me warm. After long days of scrounging for food and making meals of what we can, we sit around the fire in our home, sharing all our dreams for the future when this awful war is over and the bitter cold has finally passed. At night we curl up in our bed together, a mess of arms and legs. Sometimes I watch Han'zir get on his knees, and Drazak licks him, getting him ready with shining oil, squeezing fingers inside him to make his path easier. Then Drazak slides in, the two of them grunting with their ecstasy. Often, I can't help myself and I take Han'zir into my mouth, suckling him until he gushes and cries out our names. Drazak buries himself deep, groaning as his seed spills down Han'zir's cheeks.

But they do not speak of *whelps* again. They never empty themselves inside me. I know they're afraid of scaring me away.

The soldiers don't come back. One day in town, Han'zir learns that the war has ended. Humans stole what land they could and then the trollkin took it back in a tide of blood, until a stalemate was reached. We don't have to worry that our meager crops will be ripped away from us again.

At last, the clouds begin to part and the weather takes a turn for the better. The puppies are born, and they are sweet and small and full of life. The world warms up, and our winter tubers are ready to harvest. At last we have fresh food, and I'm certain that someday soon, the farm will be productive and well once again.

We've done it, the three of us, together.

Han'zir

When the days grow longer again and slivers of green emerge from the ground, I am overcome by relief. The future—while still uncertain—looks brighter by the moment. We have two horses to help with the work, and when the spring crops come up, we ought to be able to sell our harvest for enough to buy new chickens.

I couldn't have asked for a happier life with my mates. Even after a long day working in the field, Drazak's cock is always hungry for us. But I know we both long for something more, something we aren't willing to discuss out loud, though I can see it in his eyes as clearly as he can in mine. What if we reopened a wound and Esme ran from us again?

I don't believe she would, but I spend all my waking moments showing her what she means to me anyway. Sometimes, when we're tending vegetables, I brush my lips over her hair as I pass. When she cooks for us I always clean up afterwards, and even ask her to teach me since I'm the only one who can't seem to cook a piece of meat without burning it.

One warm spring night, while we all sit around the fire playing with Keva's puppies, Esme taps my shoulder. I lean into her, listening closely.

"What is it, heart?" I ask, wondering if perhaps she's cold, and I bring her against my side. Drazak scoots closer, squeezing me around the shoulders.

"Remember... a long time ago?" she begins, tentative. She picks one of the puppies up and squeezes it, kissing it on the nose. "When you wanted whelps?"

I freeze up. Has she been reading our thoughts? Can she feel how much I burn—*sear*—with the need to fill her up, to plant a seed in her and watch it take root? How badly I want to see her full and ripe with us, to enjoy our small orcs or trolls toddling around the farm?

"What of them?" Drazak finally says, as tense as I am.

Esme worries her lip between her teeth. "Do you... do you still want them?"

My throat closes. Is this some sort of test? I glance at Drazak, and I can see the same thoughts in his yellow eyes. What's the right answer?

The best I can do is tell her the truth. I will never lie to Esme.

"Yes," I finally say, not releasing my hold on her. "Always." My cock gets warm just thinking of Drazak sliding into her, filling her, his essence dripping into her womb and finding purchase there many times over. She is our mate, after all—we were created this way. All my cock seeks is to watch her swell up round and then, when the time is right, enjoy as her big breasts feed our small, helpless whelps.

"And you?" Esme asks, tilting her head at Drazak. He looks just as thunderstruck, and he struggles for the words.

Finally, they come out quiet and strained. "Yes. More than anything."

When a small smile tilts her lips, I can finally breathe again.

"Then we should try." She leans into me, and I gasp for air as I bring her close against my chest. "I think we have everything we need."

Drazak's deep-throated growl takes us both by surprise. He gets to his feet abruptly, then stands over her, offering his hand. Esme takes it, and he hauls her up into his arms. He kisses her, hard and hungrily, grabbing her ass and thrusting his hips against hers. Our human mate gasps in surprise.

I see. She has lit a fire in him, one that burns so bright it might fill us all up with flames.

ESME

That night, my troll and my orc are in a marvelous mood. They lay me on the bed together, forbidding me from moving as they lavish attention on me. Han'zir is quite horny tonight, and before long he's begging to put his cock in me. The idea of a new baby has brought something to life in him that tells me he will make a wonderful father.

But first, he devours the place between my legs, making me shudder and drip onto his face while Drazak lavishes attention on his body. Then Han'zir slides into me, groaning as his cock finds where it belongs. He's almost lost to his pleasure, the way he tends to get. I sit astride his lap as he brings me down hard, sinking as much of himself as he can inside me.

"Esme," he moans, sweat beading on his forehead. I can see him through his face, all of him. His eyes redden as he draws a hand down my cheek. I know then that our hearts are wrapped so tightly around one another that he will always feel what I do, and I will always feel what he does.

Drazak's hands travel down my body, from my breasts to my hips, and around to cup my ass. "I need to be inside you, too," he whispers in my ear, and a full-body shiver travels through me. I know what he wants: for all of our three pieces to fit together again. We've never done it with all of him inside me—usually, they only tease me while I'm so full, just putting in a few fingers, but I know I can take him.

"Please," I murmur, and Drazak's breath hitches. He reaches between us, to the place where Han'zir's cock thrusts in and out of me, and coats his fingers in our juices, using them to test me. He teases the puckered hole between my cheeks, widening it with one digit, and then two. I fall against Han'zir, already overcome by the pressure of his cock and Drazak's hand inside me. My moans become cries as my orc widens that taut ring of muscle further, and then positions himself behind me, slathering his cock with oil to ease his way.

When the fat head of Drazak's cock prods at my second entrance, I let out a sharp cry. It's tight and painful at first, but my orc is patient. Han'zir pants as he pauses his frantic thrusting, watching what Drazak is about to do.

"We'll fill her up quite full," Han'zir remarks, bringing his hands up to my breasts. "Ah, these are so beautiful." He kisses me hard as Drazak finally slips in. I moan as it widens me, stretching me, forcing me to give. With Han'zir's cock inside me already, the sensation of Drazak filling me up, too, is almost more than I can bear. I cry out, and Drazak slows his invasion, leaning over me to breathe in my ear.

"Relax, sweet one," he whispers, thrusting shallowly, and the pain and pleasure meld together into an indescribable feeling. His hands travel my body, caressing me like something precious and fragile. I know then who he is, how I've always been meant for him. It feels like I'm being consumed by them both. As Drazak tests me, Han'zir starts to move again, and my troll lets out a strangled groan.

"She's so tight," he mutters helplessly. Then Drazak slips the rest of the way inside, and I feel as if I might simply break apart with the ferocious pleasure that overwhelms me. Drazak's arms wind around my chest, holding me steady as he always does. My sturdy orc who protects me, whose huge, bright soul peeks out from behind his stern face. As he settles in place, he groans and holds me close.

"Esme," he murmurs, kissing my ear, my neck, my shoulder. Together they stroke in and out of me, my orc and my troll, and I am whimpering and sobbing with my bliss. Here, filled by them, everything is right where it should be. I can taste who they are, what they're made of as we all climb toward that marvelous place in the sky. Han'zir thrusts deeper, his head thrown back as he swells up thick inside me, and I think I might just explode. When he bursts, I can't hold it back any longer, and my scream fills up the whole clay house. Drazak gasps, and his breaths come ragged.

"Fuck," he moans, burying himself deep, his tusks scraping my back. "You take our cocks so well, my gorgeous girl." And then he unleashes, making me peak all over again.

By the time we're finished, I am a shivering mass of sensation, their seed leaking from my very pores. Drazak brings me into his arms, where he holds me tight, kissing my forehead. Han'zir curls up behind him, draped over Drazak's shoulder.

"I wonder which one of us will plant the whelp?" he asks, smoothing a hand down my hair. "I got a head start."

Drazak yawns. "I don't know, but I'm excited to find out."

My body trembles at the idea.

CHAPTER 18

DRAZAK

I've never smiled so much in all my life. With summer on the way, Han'zir is playful and bright, and I even catch him fucking Esme out in the field, bringing her down on his cock while she moans. He is thrilled by the idea of whelps, and I secretly hope that his seed takes first so he might enjoy a sweet youngster who looks like him. If we're able to achieve what we're hoping, he will teach them to play with their whole hearts, and I bask in the idea of him holding them in his arms. And Esme's kindness, her need to love with all she has, will make her the most wonderful mother they could ask for.

And I will protect them all, until the day I die. At night, I bring my troll and my human in close and hold them tight so they know they're safe. I make sure we have enough coin for all the fresh food and new clothes we need, and I have sturdy shoes made for Esme in town.

She gets tired in the evenings more and more often, and has occasionally begun to retch up perfectly good food. Han'zir is immensely concerned, asking if we ought to fetch a healer, but Esme's still our secret, at least for now. Since the war is over, we may not have to hide her forever.

I'm chuffed, though. One night I pull Esme onto my lap and wrap my arms tight around her. "I haven't seen your blood on my cock in some time," I murmur into her throat, the lump under my pants already pressing eagerly at her soft butt. "I wonder why?"

She turns this over in her mind, not understanding.

"Do you think?" Han'zir asks with a gasp. His eyes light up like stars. "Did we do it?"

"Do what?" Esme asks. I trail a hand from her collar to her breasts, and then to her belly. I test it out with one palm and she wriggles, trying to bring my fingers under her new dress.

"Put a whelp in you," I whisper into her ear, and she shudders all over. I breathe in her smell, and a warmth settles in me as I consider that she's carrying a small creature we all made together.

"Oh. Perhaps so." Esme grins a wide, warm grin. "I wonder what it'll be?"

Han'zir kneels in front of her, kissing her lips, then smoothing a hand over her soft stomach. "We'll find out," he hums, while I cup her breasts, plucking her nipples over her dress and making her squirm with pleasure.

"But first," I say, "we should celebrate."

After we gorge ourselves on food by the fire, Han'zir brings out his drum and taps out a rhythm while I take Esme by the hand. I pull her against me, leaning my head down over her shoulder as we move to the beat.

"Esme," I murmur, my tusks dragging over her skin. "My hope." She tangles her hands in my hair, nuzzling her nose into my cheek.

Then I release her so we can dance around the fire.

HAN'ZIR

We've done it. Our sweet mate is full with us, and I couldn't be happier. As her belly swells—and so do her marvelous breasts—we both grow even hungrier for her. I love to see her atop Drazak, swallowing his delectable cock, and I lie down to lick her sweet cunt as he slicks in and out of her. When she's tired, it's me and my orc, and I pull him onto my lap and bury myself in his tight, perfect ass. News of the coming whelp has turned me into an animal, and I can't get enough of him, rolling his balls in my hands and going off a little too early when I think that it might be his seed sprouting inside her.

As always, he's our steady hand, our guardian. He works in the fields until sweat pours down his flawless body, and I can't resist him. It feels like every day is better than the one before it as my precious plants sprout from the ground, spreading their leaves and growing as ripe as Esme. Watching the puppies get bigger, I think of our whelp opening its sweet eyes, learning how to walk and talk. It puts an extra spring in my step to think of our sunny farm full of our brood as I merrily make my way to the house for dinner.

Drazak has mastered a new, even spicier pepper that sells quite well at the market. We've been his taste-testers, as miserable as it makes me, but I can't deny the coin it brings in. Inside, my mates are squabbling over how best to cook up the chicken we slaughtered, and I simply sit at the table and watch them with a stupid grin on my face.

That night, I fill the tub myself while they work and build a warm fire underneath it. When we're through with dinner, I call Esme over.

"I have a present," I tell her, sidling up behind her to sweep my hands down her round body. Eyebrows raised, she follows me out to the bath, where she takes off her clothes and I lift her up into the warm water. Then I crawl in with her and bring her feet in my lap to rub them thoroughly, until her head has fallen back and her eyes are closed. Drazak laughs one of his booming laughs when he finds us out there, Esme asleep in the tub, and adds more logs to the fire.

It is, truly, the best life I could have asked for.

Esme

I am rather fat by the time the cool weather returns, and though I do my best to carry my share of the work, my mates are not so keen. They baby me to the point that I have to slap their hands away and insist I can do *some* things on my own. Their delicacy ends when we are in the bedroom, though. Since they discovered they can both have me at once, they are like puppies themselves, unable to contain their excitement. Still, I am often sore and my body aches. I'm growing bigger every day, and I don't know when it will end. When I get too sensitive, Han'zir licks me sweetly while Drazak takes him from behind, and I'm glad they can fulfill one another's needs.

I'm crouched over a vegetable stalk, picking off leaves that have acquired a strange mold, when the pain strikes me. I double over and cry out, and Han'zir is there in a moment. He helps me to my feet, but I double over again as another searing bolt races through me.

"Drazak!" Han'zir hollers across the farm, and my orc comes running. "It's here!"

I sob and scream, and yet, despite the agony that threatens to rip me to pieces, our daughter emerges anyway. Han'zir lets out a *whoop!* as he helps bring her out, and I'm ragged and gasping with a tear-streaked face when he kneels down beside me. Drazak's eyes go wide when he sees the little human baby in Han'zir's arms, skin the same color as mine with a smooth head. He rubs his chin.

"Human?" he asks, baffled. Then a huge grin spreads across his face.

I hold out my arms and Han'zir gently lays her in them. Then they lie down at my sides as she latches around my nipple.

"I wonder what the next one will be," Han'zir says, one eyebrow arched.

"Shut up," I tell him. "After all that?" He falls silent, but Drazak just laughs.

Our daughter grows quickly. Keva and the younger dogs watch over her as she lies in her basket, and I pause frequently during our day's work to feed her. Han'zir's favorite activity is to put her in his lap, the baby's tiny fingers wrapped around one of his big ones, and hold her up so she can practice walking. Drazak, however, is the only one who seems able to get her to go to sleep. The moment the baby's in his arms, she's off to dreamland, and then Drazak's stuck with her.

As our harvest comes in abundant and plentiful, we're able to sell enough to buy a cow, a bull, and a few chickens. Even the next time the winter settles in, the farm is radiant and bright, and we have all the stores we need to be comfortable.

At night, while the baby sleeps—or doesn't sleep, which is often—my orc and my troll hold me tight, and our constellation glows as brightly as ever. Han'zir murmurs as he finds me in the bed, his eyes glittering with mischief.

"Ready for the next one?" he whispers to me as the noise wakes Drazak up. My orc turns over, grumbling, but when he squeezes my nipples, milk drips out and he licks it up.

"Yes," I say, gasping as my troll draws me up onto my hands and knees. He sucks on Drazak's cock until it's thick and hard, and then guides it inside me, spreading my swollen lower lips while

Drazak fills me up to bursting. I can feel the moment Han'zir enters him from behind because our orc cries out and bucks, driving himself even deeper. It feels as if we might all converge, our three hearts melding into one.

When we're sated, Han'zir pulls me into his arms, murmuring little praises while Drazak curls up around us both. We fall asleep that way, a tangled mess of limbs, right where we belong.

Thank you for reading!

If you enjoyed this book, please consider leaving a review! Written reviews help indie authors like me reach new readers.

The next adventure

There's even more coming in the Trollkin Lovers universe! Next up is *Finding the Troll's Heart,* an age gap romance about our favorite one-tusked corporal.

Join My Newsletter!

For all the latest regarding books, and to get a FREE novella that takes place in the Trollkin Lovers universe, sign up for my newsletter!

www.LyonneRiley.com

For even more stories and lots of NSFW artwork, come check me out on Patreon!

www.Patreon.com/LyonneRiley

About the Author

Lyonne Riley published her first book at age five, which was written on tiny sheets of notebook paper, and she insisted on giving a copy to everyone she knew. She's been writing ever since, from fan fiction in her teen years to original fiction as an adult. After a stint in traditional publishing, she discovered what she truly wanted to write: very smutty stories about monstrous orcs and the little humans they worship.

Now she lives in the middle of nowhere with her dogs and spouse, writing sexy fairy tales.

facebook.com/lyonneriley

x.com/lyonneriley

instagram.com/lyonneriley

amazon.com/stores/Lyonne-Riley/author/B0C57K1NM3

Acknowledgments

I would like to thank everyone involved in helping me through the process of putting out this book. I can't say enough how much I appreciate the help and encouragement of the people around me—especially Amber, who told me I could do this in the first place.

Huge thank you to Rowan Woodcock for the gorgeous cover illustration. To my critique partners, Kass, Sara, Ash and Ruth, who gave me phenomenal feedback: You all make this possible. And of course, my amazing spouse, who has always supported my dreams—and given me lots of inspiration for my characters' sexy adventures.

I couldn't have done this without the expertise of my fellow self-published romance authors. Thank you for inviting me into your circles and helping me through this process.

And thank you to my readers, who gave this book a shot.